Third Term at L'Etoile

School
for
Stars

Also by Holly and Kelly Willoughby

First Term at L'Etoile
Second Term at L'Etoile

Third Term at L'Etoile

School for Stars

Holly & Kelly Willoughby

Orion
Children's Books

First published in Great Britain in 2014
by Orion Children's Books
a division of the Orion Publishing Group Ltd
Orion House
5 Upper St Martin's Lane
London WC2H 9EA
An Hachette UK Company

1 3 5 7 9 10 8 6 4 2

Printed in Great Britain by Clays Ltd, St Ives plc

ISBN 978 1 4440 0815 9

www.orionbooks.co.uk

For aspiring L'Etoilettes everywhere who dare to dream and who have the courage to make those dreams come true. Reach for the Stars and you might just grab a glittering handful!

Contents

Welcome back, Story-seeker, to the third term at L'Etoile.

How we've missed you over the Easter Holidays! You'll be happy to know that Molly, Maria, Pippa and the rest of the L'Etoile gang are back for more friendship, fun and mischief.

As they reach the end of their first year at L'Etoile, the girls are filled with excitement and apprehension about what lies ahead. Molly's got that huge Warner Brothers film audition, the dreaded Lucifette is back from LA with an even more hideous sidekick to stir up a whole heap of trouble, the pressure's on for the first years to raise more money than ever before at the L'Etoile annual charity event and don't forget the nightmare of exam week.

Will our fabulous friends get through another term without ending up in hot water? There's only one way to find out, Story-seeker, so what are you waiting for? Turn the page and get yourselves back to L'Etoile!

Love,
Holly and Kelly Willoughby x

1

One Good Turn Deserves Another

Molly stood shivering with cold and nerves at the top of the casting studio steps in London. She couldn't believe the day had finally arrived for her big audition for a Warner Brothers film.

'Come o-o-n, Mimi!' she said to herself, breathing out a cloud of chilly morning air. 'Where *are* you?'

Much to Molly's dismay the ever-obliging Eddie, her dad's chauffeur, had dropped Molly off at the studio only twenty minutes earlier, and then, at Maria's request, had whisked her away on a mystery errand. Molly was totally fed up. She always needed Maria near her to steady her nerves when she was about to face something really important or scary.

How could her twin sister leave her this morning, of all mornings?

Jiggling on the spot, she checked her watch for the millionth time. 'I can't believe she's been gone this long. I bet she's off to get some pointless cable or adapter or something for one of her many gadgets,' she said out loud. Just as Molly was about to lose her temper and start ranting about responsibilities and priorities, she was distracted by a shadow shuffling in the doorway at the end of the studio block.

Trying her best not to look as if she was staring, she started pacing up and down the steps so that she could get a better look. She was sure it must be one of those urban foxes she'd been reading about. Suddenly a large, round, hairy face peered out from a pile of blankets and newspapers. *Oh my gosh, it's not a fox at all! He must be absolutely freezing*, she thought to herself. If she felt cold after only twenty or so minutes hanging around outside, how must he feel after an entire night? Not caring that she was so obviously staring now, she watched the man go about his business, and was shocked to see how passer-by after passer-by walked past him without even looking in his direction. It was as though he was invisible, as insignificant as a dirty old carrier bag lying in the gutter. Suddenly Molly gave an enormous sneeze, and the man looked right at her.

'Bless you!' he grunted in a low, gravelly voice.

Molly was mortified. How could this poor man with nothing still be so gracious?

'Thank you, sir,' she answered loud enough for him to hear her.

All of a sudden, the Fitzfoster Bentley pulled up in front of the studio steps.

'Moll! What are you still standing outside for?' Maria asked urgently as she threw open the car door. 'Get in at once! You've already got the sniffles and it's hardly a summer's day out here. Think of your voice.'

'Mimi, where have you been? Five minutes you said! That was nearly half an hour ag—' Molly stopped dead in her tracks as she saw the gorgeous, fresh-faced Pippa emerging from the other side of the car.

'You heard your sister, Molly Fitzfoster! Now do as you're told. You have the audition of a lifetime ahead of you.'

'Pippa!' Molly squealed, running over to hug her. 'What are you . . . how did you . . . but what about . . . ?'

'Sur-prise!' Maria said, relieved that Molly was no longer cross with her for being late. 'You've been so nervous about today, Moll, that Pippa and I thought two heads might be better than one to calm you down this morning, so we've been plotting all week how to get her here in time.'

'Oh, Molly, it's totally my fault we're late,' said Pippa. 'My first two trains were cancelled for some rubbish reason or another. I knew you'd both be hopping mad, but I couldn't do a thing about it. Poor Mum had to listen to me moaning the whole way.'

Molly smiled her biggest smile, happy to have her favourite girls with her on this important day. 'Oh, don't worry about that now. I was just feeling sorry for myself. I can't tell you how wicked it is to have you both here. Even my butterflies have butterflies!' She clutched her tummy and winced.

'Poor Sally was desperate to come along too, Moll,' Maria said. 'But we just couldn't risk her being seen as part of Team Molly and bumping into Lucifette at the audition.'

'Don't remind me!' Molly groaned. 'I still can't believe she's managed to wangle herself the same casting. WATC?'

We're sure you're used to Molly's little Mollyisms by now, Story-seeker, but just in case, WATC = what are the chances.

'Have you seen the little Hollywood witch yet?' Pippa asked, looking glum at the thought of her first run-in with Lucinda since exposing her as a complete fraud in front of everyone at the Christmas Gala two terms ago.

'Not yet, thank goodness, but I'll bet she's on her way, bringing those thunderous black clouds with her,' Molly answered, looking up at the cluster of rain clouds making their way across the blue skies above the studio. Pippa and Maria giggled.

Lucinda's return from LA had been playing on the girls' minds. They were all dreading it. Not because they were scared of her . . . well, at least the twins weren't, but they couldn't speak for the rest of their year group. No one could face another term of treading on eggshells, waiting for it to be their turn to be bullied by Lucinda. The second term at L'Etoile, when Lucinda had been in LA, had been such a happy time for them. They'd had fun, without any of the spiteful misery.

'Come on then, *Mollywood*. Let's get this show on the road. You can't put this off forever,' said Maria with a wink.

As Molly turned to take her sister's hand, secretly loving *Mollywood* as a nickname, she remembered the homeless man, and looked over to see him watching them.

'Just a minute,' Molly said. 'There's something I've got to do quickly.'

She raced down the steps to the car and tapped on the window.

'Eddie, have you got any money that I could borrow, please? I'll pay you back, I promise.'

Eddie popped open the glove compartment and, as luck would have it, a ten-pound note came fluttering out.

'Perfect!' Molly said and bolted over the road to Café Graceybelle.

'What *is* she up to, Maria?' asked Pippa, confused. One minute they were catching up and next, Molly had run off on a mission!

Maria smiled. She could read her sister like a book and as soon as she'd witnessed Molly lock eyes with that man, she knew exactly what she was up to.

'You'll see, Pips. You're about to see why Molly is our mother's daughter,' she said.

Every moment she had without her girls, Linda Fitzfoster spent fundraising for various charities, Story-seeker. She truly had the kindest heart and used her family's wealth and influence for those in need.

Moments later, Molly came out of Café Graceybelle with a large steaming cup and a bulging paper bag. Being careful not to slop any tea, she made a beeline for the man. She slowed down as she got closer to him. After all, he was a stranger and you couldn't be too careful. But Molly couldn't help herself. She just wanted to try and help him warm up, and the fact that he'd said *bless you* when she'd sneezed gave her every confidence that there was a nice person underneath all that street dirt.

'E-e-excuse me, sir,' she said timidly. 'I wasn't sure if you have sugar in tea so there's some sachets in the bag – and something to eat too.'

The man seemed to have difficulty focusing on her, as though his eye-sight was bad. Eventually he smiled up at her and took the bag.

'Two sugars,' he said gruffly, taking a slurp of tea. And 'Ahhhhh,' as he devoured a crumpet dripping with butter.

Molly was slightly surprised at how tubby he was for someone who seemed to be so hungry, and thought how ordinary he might look after a shower and in some clean clothes. Feeling a bit braver, she asked his name.

'Calum,' said the man in the same gruff way.

'It's very nice to meet you, Calum,' Molly said. She'd been thinking how it must feel if no one even cared enough to ask your name. As she turned to walk away, she looked back and gently placed the change from the ten-pound note on his blanket.

'It's not much, I know. But might do for a few more crumpets. Good luck, Calum,' she said and ran off to join Maria and Pippa.

'Molly, you are too cute!' Maria said.

'Yes, that was such a lovely thing you did. You've inspired me. I'm going to try and be much more thoughtful towards others this term,' Pippa said.

'And to think you'll be ten pounds down on your next *www.looklikeastar.com* order! Now that's what I call a sacrifice!' Maria joked.

Molly blushed and swiped her sister playfully with her script, secretly feeling very pleased with herself.

All of a sudden a big black limousine came careering round the corner and screeched to a halt.

'LU-CI-FETTE!' the trio groaned in unison, taking a step back into the shadows so they could watch without being seen. The three girls shook their heads in despair as they watched the little Hollywood princess step out of the car.

'Oh my days, look at her hair!' Molly blurted out. 'She looks like a skunk with those platinum blonde streaks. I've never seen anything like it bef—' But before she could say another word, the long-suffering Marciano driver opened the other passenger door to what could only be described as Lucinda's evil twin. The second person had the same dreadful streaked hair-do, but was shorter and had a meaner face than Lucinda – if that was possible!

'Someone tell me I'm not actually seeing what I'm seeing! Are there really two of them?' Pippa gasped. 'Has she been cloned? Is that what they're doing in LA these days?'

'I think, girls, you're looking at – to quote lovely Sally – the *horror-hog*, that is, Lavinia Wright, daughter of the infamous American talk-show host, Tallulah Wright. Sally told us at the end of last term. Don't you remember?' Maria said calmly.

'I remember it. I'm looking at it. But I don't believe it. At least I don't think I want to believe it!' Pippa said with a gulp.

Pippa, Story-seeker, was secretly terrified of Lucinda since the Christmas Gala exposure and had been dreading her return. Seeing not one, but two Lucindas arrive had almost given her a heart attack. She knew she had to get a grip before term started, or they'd smell her fear and take her down!

'Oy!' came a booming voice from down the street.

Molly grabbed her sister's shoulder in shock as they saw Calum swaying towards them, waving his fists. He'd been drenched from head to toe by muddy water as the Marciano car had sped off.

'Oy, I said!' Calum shouted again, pointing to his soaking wet clothes. 'Do you know how cold it gets, sleeping outside overnight? Who do you think you are?'

'Do you hear something, Lavinia darling?' Lucinda rudely cut across Calum.

'I most certainly cannot *hear* anything, Lucie sweetie, but I can certainly SMELL something!' Lavinia replied, looking directly at Calum and holding her nose. 'Come on, darling, let's get inside, before we catch some disease or other from this tramp.'

And with that, the two disgusting brats swooshed around on their badly fitting kitten-heels and headed for the steps.

The twins and Pippa were astounded. Maria had to physically hold Molly back from jumping to Calum's defence.

'Not now, Molly, this is his battle. You can't fight them all – especially not this morning. Quick, slip inside before those two get there and find a quiet spot to get your head straight for your audition . . . we're right behind you, Moll . . . GO!' Maria ordered.

As Molly disappeared into the studio, she and Pippa shrank back even further against the wall so as not to come into direct contact with Lucinda and Lavinia. They just couldn't face it. Not yet. Not until they'd had an entire car journey to L'Etoile to dissect and discuss exactly what they were dealing with – now that the enemy had doubled.

'We'll be ready for them, Pips. Don't you worry,' Maria said confidently, noticing Pippa's distress.

'What?' Pippa said, distracted.

'Lucifette and Lavatory,' Maria said with a giggle, amused by her new nickname for Lavinia. 'They won't get the better of us, I promise.'

Pippa grinned for the first time since the limo had arrived.

'Luci and Lavi! Love it! Bring it on, Mimi!'

2

All Aboard for L'Etoile

As the Fitzfoster Bentley made its way through the streets of London, bound for L'Etoile, its three young passengers bounced away gently on the back seat. Maria and Pippa had been so busy gossiping about how they were going to handle Lucinda and Lavinia, they'd only just noticed that Molly wasn't actually asleep, but staring, wide-eyed, out of the window.

'Oh, Molly, we thought we'd let you sleep for a bit — but you're not sleeping at all. It's not like you to be so quiet. You've not said a word about your audition. What happened? Did it go well, do you think?' asked Maria, always concerned when her chatterbox sister suddenly stopped chattering.

'The truth is, girls, I've absolutely no idea how it went. It was so top-secret in there. You'd have thought I was auditioning to become a spy in the secret service, not for a kid's film. They even gave me a whole new script when I walked in, so all that stressing about the original one they sent me was for nothing! And to top that, I couldn't even see the people I was talking to. They sat me on my own in a big, white room with just a chair, a table and a camera – you know, like in one of those movie interrogation scenes, where the detectives are gathered behind a big mirror looking in, but the suspect can't see them,' said Molly.

'That's a bit unfair, isn't it?' said Pippa. 'They hardly put you at ease did they? And how can they expect you to do your best with a character you've only just been given?'

'I've no idea. All the director said was that the part had to be lived and breathed by the actress, not just acted. He said that I was being judged on my every movement, not just on how well I delivered my lines. He told me to be myself and that they'd know immediately when they'd found the right person.'

'Blimey, could they be any more cryptic?' Maria said. 'No wonder you're confused, poor thing. I think they've totally flummoxed you.'

'I don't suppose that new script gave any idea what the film is about, did it?' asked Pippa.

'Nope! I still haven't got a flipping clue!' Molly answered, shaking her head. 'And the weirdest thing of all was one minute I was saying my lines, and the next they told me to burst into tears . . . just like that . . . for no reason.'

'Nightmare! I have enough trouble crying for real, let alone crying on demand!' Maria said.

'Well, I was worried, but suddenly I got this image in my head of poor Calum, soaking wet and freezing cold, and I couldn't stop crying,' Maria answered, her eyes filling up again.

'Oh Molly, you are sweet. Calum will be fine. You did your best for him this morning,' Pippa said, stretching over to squeeze Molly's hand.

'Anyway, WATC of Lucifette crying on demand? *Little Miss Heart of Stone* wouldn't have had a hope of producing any real emotion. They'll have seen through her straight away. You mark my words, *Mollywood*,' chuckled Maria.

'I like *Mollywood*, Mimi. Consider it an approved nickname.' Molly smiled wearily and turned back to face the window. 'If it's OK with you girls, I think I might actually try to get an hour's sleep before we get to school. I am absolutely pooped! It's been quite a day!'

'I might join you,' Pippa said. 'I think we're going to need all the energy we can muster to get through this term. Luci and Lavi are going to bring more misery than I care to think about . . . '

' . . . not to mention the dreaded exams,' Molly piped up, her eyes closed. 'How will we ever top last term for excitement? You can only top a prince with a king, and I'm not at all bothered about meeting a king!'

'What are you two like?' Maria exclaimed. 'Cheer up and stop worrying about everything. Let's have a little more enthusiasm and a little less doom and gloom. It'll be fun, you'll see! Who knows, we might just have the best time ever!'

3

Reunited

'WAIT!' Maria said, throwing her arm across her sister and Pippa like a bodyguard. 'I think there's someone in our room . . . listen!'

The three girls held their breath.

'Pleeease don't let it be Luci and Lavi . . . not already,' Pippa whispered.

'Would you just look at us three idiots creeping around in the corridor, outside our own bedroom. You've got me at it now!' Maria snapped. She was slightly annoyed with herself for feeling so nervous. 'We've got to get a grip!' And with that, she karate-kicked their door so hard, it nearly flew off its hinges.

'SALLY!' Molly squealed and ran over to where

Sally was standing as though she'd been electrocuted.

'Girls!' Sally screeched. 'You scared me! Is that some sort of secret code to enter the room or something? You nearly took the door off, Maria.'

'Sorry, Sally. It's these two panicky-bottoms. They've got all three of us so churned up about the return of Lucifette, they're turning me into a nervous wreck. My logic is all over the place. I never even considered it might be you in here,' Maria said, annoyed with herself. She gave Sally a big hug.

'Oh, Sally, it's sooo good to see you. How've you been? Love the dress, BTW . . .

BTW = by the way, Story-seeker.

. . . Totes *fashion*! Is it new?' asked Molly, kindly.

Sally blushed, so delighted that Molly had noticed. She'd been doing all sorts of odd jobs over the Easter holidays so that she could make some money to buy a couple of dresses for her new start with the trendy Fitzfoster twins.

'Yes, Molly. Do you like it? I ordered it from *www. looklikeastar.com* — I remembered how many lovely things you get from there.'

'Of course it is! How jealous am I? I think I saw

that one on there but it was so popular it sold out in seconds. How clever of you, Sally. It really suits you.'

'I'd watch your back if I were you, Miss Sudbury. You should know that any fashion item Molly admires, be it clothing, shoes or accessories, she'll get her paws on eventually, so don't be surprised if it goes walkabout,' Maria joked.

'Oh, you're welcome to borrow it anytime!' Sally said, beaming with pride and feeling like part of the gang.

'Likewise!' said Molly. 'We share everything round here . . . isn't that right, Pips?'

'I draw the line at knickers though, if you don't mind. Quite like to keep those to myself!' she giggled.

'Talking of knickers – I'm utterly convinced there should be a law against enormous navy-blue knickers!' Molly grimaced, holding up a brand-new pack of school uniform pants, which they had to wear under their new lightweight summer dresses. 'And don't get me started on this polyester blue-and-white-checked dress! Besides the fact that we look like Dorothy from the *Wizard of Oz,* when I tried it on in the shop, the skirt part was so static it stuck to my legs and looked like a pair of shorts!' Molly continued, genuinely horrified at the thought of being forced to wear anything other than pure cotton during the summer months. 'I'm shocked at L'Etoile selecting such poor-quality fabric, to be honest.'

'Oh, it's only for one term, Moll,' Pippa said, loving Molly's passion for fashion. 'I tell you what . . . why don't you wear your own nice knickers underneath the navy granny-bashers? That might help you feel slightly more normal.'

'Girls, be serious! It's for school, not the catwalk. It's meant to be hideous!' Maria exclaimed, delighted at the idea of not having to go through the drama of finding something *Molly-approved* to wear every morning!

As the four friends unpacked, as neatly as they always did on the first day of term, knowing that their drawers and cupboards would descend into utter chaos before long, they gossiped about their holidays.

'Sounds like Easter at the Fitzfosters' is the biggest chocolate-fest ever!' Sally said, her mouth watering at the thought of giant-sized chocolate bunny rabbits.

'Don't worry – you haven't missed out,' Maria said, throwing open a brand-new trunk. 'We brought it all with us. What do you say to that, girls?'

'OH MY . . . ' Sally said.

'Supercalifragilisticexpialidocious!' Pippa exclaimed.

'What?' Maria, Molly and Sally said together, followed by a fit of giggles.

Pippa couldn't actually believe she'd said that out loud. It was one of those things – thanks to watching *Mary Poppins* over and over when she was little – that she'd said all her life whenever she saw something extraordinary. It's just until now, she'd managed to say it under her breath rather than out loud and risk becoming a laughing stock.

'Well, it worked for *Mary Poppins* when she didn't know what else to say,' Pippa replied, knowing she was digging herself an even bigger hole.

Maria grinned. 'Before you commit total social suicide, Pippa, shall we just pretend that never happened?'

'Yes thank you, Maria, that would be extremely noble of you,' Pippa said, relieved but suspecting that Maria would no doubt use this knowledge at some point to force her to get up to some Fitzfoster mischief.

'Changing the subject completely . . . ' Sally said, leaping to Pippa's rescue. 'Er, can we discuss the fact that you girls are now in fact national heroines? Thanks for emailing to give me the heads-up before the

Easter weekend article went out in *Gazelle* magazine, BTW. You should have seen Lucifette's face when she saw that picture of you girls with old Ruby and Miss Hart splashed across the front cover. And I couldn't resist winding her up further by telling her I knew all about it when she hadn't heard! She didn't even hang around to ask me how, and as a result the magazine is now ashes in the kitchen fireplace!'

'That's brilliant!' said Pippa, picturing Lucinda's face.

'Not sure you haven't shot yourself in the foot a bit, though. Does she even know you're sharing a room with us yet?' said Molly, who could tell that, for all her bravado, Sally was still terrified of Lucinda.

'She does, but she doesn't know I'm ecstatically happy about it. She thinks I've been kicked out of our old room to make space for that horror-hog, Lavinia Wright. When I told her I was being teamed up with you three she said it's everything I deserve and more. She thinks it's a punishment!' Sally answered.

'Oh, let her think what she wants, darling,' Molly said. 'What's important is that you're here with us now and we'll look after you. You're not to worry about a thing, Sally – tell her, Mimi.'

'Right!' said Maria. 'Not a thing!'

'I know what we could do to take our mind off everything,' Pippa said, flicking through one of the twins' twenty copies of *Gazelle*. 'Let's finish unpacking, put a padlock on that chocolate chest, and then pay this little treasure a visit!'

She held up the magazine and staring out at them was the little pink nose and black, furry face of their beloved Twinkle, on her totally OTT (*OTT = over the top, Story-seeker*) throne-bed guarding the Lost Rose.

Twinkle, Story-seeker, if you remember, is their beloved rescue dog – well, almost their beloved dog; they had to pass their rescue mission on to the school caretaker, Mr Hart, to complete, rather than keeping her hidden at Garland – but you'll have to cast your mind back to the girls' second-term adventures to hear that story again.

'Oh, yes, let's!' exclaimed Molly. 'I'm dying for a cuddle. I wonder if she's grown? What if she doesn't even remember who we are?'

'Only one way to find out!' Maria said, jumping up. 'Come on, girls, we can sneak down for half an hour. It's too early for anyone to miss us. Half of our year hasn't even arrived.'

'And where are you four off to in such a hurry?' a voice called out.

The quartet stopped in their tracks and turned to see the smiling face of Miss Hart.

'Don't tell me you're up to your old tricks already? The term hasn't even begun!' she said, raising an eyebrow.

'Miss Hart!' said Pippa, turning towards her mentor. 'Did you have a lovely Easter? What did you think of *Gazelle*? Isn't it exciting?'

'So many questions, ladies. But I'll stick to my original query if you don't mind. Where are you off to? Shouldn't you be at Garland unpacking for the new term?'

'Oh, we've done that, Miss Hart. We're actually going to find Twinkle – to check she's doing a good job of guarding the Lost Rose,' Maria said in her best, business-like tone.

'I see. Well, if you're sure you're ready for supper then I don't see why you shouldn't do that. You'll notice lots of changes to the entrance hall. The builders have been busy at work, preparing for the summer mystery tours. In fact, I'd like to know your thoughts when you have a moment, girls. Perhaps you'd drop me an email later, Maria?'

'Certainly, Miss,' said Maria, always delighted to be asked her opinion on anything.

Molly, who hadn't said a word, had been trying to work out what was different about their favourite teacher. She was renowned for noticing absolutely everything to do with a person's appearance but in this case she just couldn't put her finger on it. Wait a minute – her finger! That was it!

'Miss Hart, Miss Hart!' she squealed with excitement. 'Congratulations! How wonderful. When did it happen? How romantic. May I see the ring, Miss?'

Helen Hart was astounded that the girls should have noticed so quickly.

When would everyone learn, Story-seeker, that these girls never missed a trick?

'Why, thank you, Molly. How very observant of you,' she answered, holding out her left hand for them to see.

By this time, Sally, Pippa and Maria had caught up with what Molly was talking about and were cooing over the beautiful diamond engagement ring sparkling on Miss Hart's finger.

'Are you kidding? I'd know one of Daddy's diamond designs anywhere,' Molly answered.

'We're so happy for you,' Pippa sang, genuinely over the moon for her teacher.

Miss Hart was touched and bemused by their reaction. 'I don't suppose I even need to tell you who it is that I'm marrying, do I?' she said. 'I expect you've got that all worked out too!'

'Mr Fuller's a very lucky man,' Maria announced confidently.

'When's the wedding?' Sally asked.

'The thirty-first of July . . . this summer, can you believe? We've so much to plan in so little time,' Miss Hart answered. 'It's been a bit of a whirlwind.'

'That's how you know it's true love, Miss,' said Molly with a dreamy look in her eyes.

And with that the girls linked arms and skipped off down the corridor singing 'Here Comes the Bride' at the top of their voices.

The girls fell silent as they approached the internal door to the entrance hall. A heady mixture of anticipation and excitement lingered in the air around them and they found themselves going the last few steps on tiptoe, just as they'd done on the night they'd made their big discovery.

'WOOF . . . WOOF . . . WOOF!' came a very loud bark from the other side of the door.

'Too late, girls . . . our cover has been blown . . . security are on to us!' Maria joked as she prised the door open a crack.

'Twinkle . . . Twin-kle, darling . . . it's only us,' Molly called softly.

'She sounds quite ferocious, doesn't she?' said Pippa. 'I'm not sure I'd have tried to get in if I didn't know what kind of dog was on the other side of that door. Good job, Twinkle-toes!'

By this time, Twinkle had leapt through the gap and was licking the girls all over.

'Ah, look how much she's missed us. I knew she would!' Molly said. She'd been so worried Twinkle might have forgotten who they were over the holidays.

'Look what they've done with the place. It looks amazing! It feels sort of magical, doesn't it . . . full of legend and ancient secrets.'

'Not so secret anymore though, eh, Agents F1 and F2?' Pippa giggled, once again staring up at the precious Lost Rose, twinkling under a spotlight. It never failed to astonish.

'WOW!' Sally gasped, staring up at the glittering ruby.

'I forgot you haven't seen it, Sal. Doesn't it take your breath away?'

'I think we've all forgotten that no one has seen it except us, a few of the teachers and the building team who've kitted this place out since last term,' said Maria, admiring the high-tech lighting. 'Wasn't it a stroke of genius, *not* putting a picture of the ruby in *Gazelle*? People will be desperate to pay to come and see it for themselves. The sketch they drew is perfect!' Pippa said.

'You're not wrong there,' said Sally. 'You *have* to see it to believe it. It's making me feel a little bit tearful, if I'm honest.'

'Ah, Sally, you're so sweet,' said Molly, hugging her. 'Just wait until you've experienced the whole mystery tour of how we found it, the book, the letter, the clues, and the treasure hunt. It's magical!'

'Hey, girls, over here,' Pippa called and the girls scurried over with Twinkle trotting happily at their heels.

To the right of the fireplace, above which L'Etoile

founder Lola Rose's portrait hung in all its glory, was a large glass display cabinet and inside lay the Hart family heirloom book, *How to Grow the Perfect Rose*. It was open at the exact page where Frank's letter had come tumbling out that night the girls had dared to steam the pages open. And there too was the letter, with the coded symbols he'd left as a kind of treasure map to anyone inquisitive and clever enough to follow.

'I still can't believe we played such a huge part in this,' Maria said.

'It was all you, Mimi,' Molly answered, squeezing her sister's hand in hers. 'You're the only real treasure-hunter here. Pippa and I were just following you.'

'No, Moll,' Maria exclaimed. 'That's simply not true. We each brought something extremely vital to the table in solving this mystery.'

'Except me,' said Sally, dropping her bottom lip. 'Maria, do you think you can find something exciting for us to do, so that I can bring something extremely vital to this term?'

'Ha!' said Maria. 'We'll certainly try, Sally Sudbury, we'll certainly try!'

4

A Heroine's Welcome

'Welcome back, L'Etoilettes, to the third and final term of another year in the history of our dear school.' As Madame Ruby paused and looked around the hall, it felt to each student there as though she was talking directly to them.

'As I know you will be only too aware, we begin the summer term of our centenary year on a tremendous high, thanks to the discovery of the mysterious Lost Rose of L'Etoile. I'm sure you will have seen the announcement in *Gazelle* magazine over the Easter weekend and know what I am talking about, but for those of you who don't, you can pick up a copy on the way out of assembly today.

'It wouldn't be fair of me to discuss this astounding discovery without mentioning the three L'Etoilettes who are responsible for solving the mystery . . .'

'Oh no, please don't . . .' Pippa whispered under her breath, breaking into a sweat. It was one thing having all eyes on you when you were on stage singing your heart out, but this was altogether different.

'Would L'Etoilettes Maria and Molly Fitzfoster and Pippa Burrows please stand up to receive a well-earned round of applause.'

Molly, who was sitting in the middle of the treasure-hunting trio, grabbed Maria's and Pippa's hands with delight and dragged them out of their seats.

Molly, as we know, Story-seeker, never has any problem with being the centre of attention.

The school erupted into whoops and cheers for the girls, who smiled and mouthed the words *thank you* to everyone who caught their eye.

'Thank you, L'Etoilettes, you may take your seats,' Madame Ruby continued.

'Take them where?' Maria whispered to Pippa, with a grin.

'If I may add a word of warning to the rest of

you, however . . . while I cannot deny that what has happened as a result of this clever trio's sleuthing is somewhat of a miracle, I would like to say that L'Etoile does *not* encourage its students to sneak around in the dead of night, dressed like assassins, hunting for lost treasure.' She paused briefly to give every student her *Ruby Warning* stare. Muffled giggles filled the room.

'So in future, L'Etoilettes, any desire you have to become the next Miss Marple or Nancy Drew should be cleared with your form tutors first! Is that understood?'

'Who knew old Ruby had such a sense of humour?' Pippa whispered to Sally.

'On a happier note, L'Etoile will open its doors for the first time to the public for summer mystery tours, as you know, but you ladies will have the opportunity this weekend to experience a mini-tour to discover the Lost Rose for yourselves. Maria Fitzfoster will be conducting these with Miss Hart and you will be called in your year groups . . . '

'Oh will I?' Maria whispered to Molly, rolling her eyes. 'That's news to me! Bloomin' cheek! Not only do I have to find the thing for everyone, I am now destined to repeat the story of how I found it forever more! Fantastic!'

'Should any of you not wish to participate . . . ' Madame Ruby continued, raising an eyebrow in Maria's direction, 'the tour is not obligatory, but I seriously recommend that you take it. We will also arrange for any family members to have access to the first week of the summer tours at a "friends and family" discounted rate.'

There was a ripple of excitement through the hall.

'Now to the other business of the summer term. On a serious note, I would remind you that the end-of-year exams are looming, so any extra study time you are able to put in will stand you in good stead. You can discuss any concerns you have with your form tutors, but as always, the examinations will be divided into academic papers and artistic performance.'

Groans flew around the room now, as the girls were brought back down to earth with a bump.

'Last, but by no means least, one of the biggest annual events is the end-of-year charity fundraiser. This is L'Etoile's opportunity to give something back to the community. Following assembly you will gather in your year groups and be asked to select a charity to raise money for. So by the time we break up for the summer holidays L'Etoile will have held six magnificent fundraisers for six deserving charities.'

Madame Ruby paused to let the students whisper their initial thoughts to each other.

'Let me guess, Moll, you want a homeless charity, right?' Maria said to her sister, taking the words out of her mouth.

'But . . . how . . . yes, actually, I do . . . ' Molly said, astonished.

Although heaven knows why, Story-seeker, we all know Maria's ten steps ahead of the game 99% of the time!

'L'Etoilettes, that's everything . . . ' Madame Ruby looked over to Miss Hart for confirmation and was immediately reminded of something.

'Oh, just one more piece of news for you all before you disappear. I am delighted to announce that my dear colleague Miss Hart is engaged to be married to Mr Emmett Fuller this summer. Congratulations, Miss Hart. We wish you every happiness in your new role as Mrs Fuller.'

The girls erupted once again into applause as Miss Hart blushed deeply.

'Poor thing,' Pippa said. 'She couldn't have gone any redder!'

'For once I don't think old Ruby actually meant to embarrass her,' said Maria. 'I think she was trying to do a nice thing. They seem to be more of a team these days since Miss Hart said she'd leave the ruby at L'Etoile.'

The girls filed out of the hall amid a mass of fellow students all firing questions at them about the night they discovered the Lost Rose. They didn't mind, but did wonder if life would ever be normal again.

Are they joking, Story-seeker? L'Etoilettes aren't destined to live normal lives!

5

Homeless Is Where the Heart Is

*K*nock, knock.

'Come in,' Mrs Spittleforth spat, as she peered over her horn-rimmed spectacles.

Dancer Heavenly Smith, from Form 1 Beta, appeared in the doorway.

'Heavens, Heavenly, dear. Is it that time already? We've barely begun registration yet. Too much chattering, you know,' she waffled. 'Are the rest of 1 Beta with you?'

Heavenly looked behind her and nodded.

'Then come on in, dear, don't stand on ceremony on our account.'

*Now you wouldn't be imagining things,
Story-seeker, if you thought you heard the whole
of form 1 Alpha take a deep breath. For the most
part, this was to be their first up close and personal
experience of Lucinda's return, along with her
new dreaded partner in crime, Lavinia Wright.*

Heavenly scurried in, followed by singers Corine, Charlotte and Autumn, Nancy and little Betsy Harris.

Then Elizabeth trotted in, linking arms with Fashion Faye, and last but not least, and as bold as brass, came Lucinda, with Lavinia and poor Sally trailing behind them. Molly wanted to jump up and pull Sally over to share her seat but didn't want to make any kind of a scene that Sally might have to explain later. There was complete silence as the whole of 1 Alpha wondered who Lucinda and Lavinia's first victim was going to be.

Lucinda's eyes wandered over each desk as she decided where she'd like to sit. Finally her gaze fixed on Belle Brown. As she began to make a move towards Belle's desk, Belle jumped up as though someone had just set fire to her socks.

'Let's make some room here, girls,' she suggested quickly to Daisy and Sofia, who were sitting either side of her.

'What a delicious idea, Bill,' Lucinda drawled, over the moon that she hadn't lost her hold over them – especially in front of Lavinia!

Maria watched in disbelief as Lucinda worked her black magic on the rest of the class.

'It's as if old Spittleforth is totally blind to what's going on here. How can she not have pulled Lucifette up for bullying poor Belle?' Maria said, frustrated.

'She's more worried about filling out that blooming register . . . look at her.'

Maria stood up, infuriated. 'Lucinda, I see you've returned from Los Angeles as delightful as you left us. May I suggest the 1 Beta girls grab the extra chairs from the back of the room and bring them over to the back two rows. 1 Alphas will squash up together on the front two.'

Lavinia's jaw dropped, shocked by Maria's confidence, Lucinda's face was a perfect shade of puce. As she opened her mouth to cut Maria down to size, Maria said, 'And you seem to have lost your memory on your travels, Lucinda. May I reintroduce you to Belle? There weren't any male students called Bill at L'Etoile, last time I checked!' and with that Maria sat back down at her desk, adrenalin pulsing through her body. Molly and Pippa both squeezed her leg under the desk to show their pride.

Before Lucinda could utter another word, Mrs Spittleforth looked up from her paperwork and began the task at hand.

'So, first years, thank you for joining our happy group. 1 Beta, you are most welcome,' she began, oblivious to the evil looks 1 Alpha, encouraged by Maria, were currently giving Lucinda and Lavinia.

'We have come together this morning to brainstorm fundraising ideas and ultimately to select the charity you feel deserves your focus. Our reason for making sure we have all this clear so early on in the term is that you will be surprised how much the exams and their build-up take over and the summer fundraiser will be upon us before you can say *distinction* – which is what I hope to be seeing in many of your results.' The room fell silent.

'Now would any of you like to start the ball rolling? Is there any particular charity close to your hearts?' Old Spittleforth continued.

'Yes,' called out a voice, a new American voice.

'Here we go,' Sally muttered.

Lavinia Wright was on her feet, determined to make an impression on her peers – and possibly not in a good way.

'Back home in Hollywood . . . where I am from . . .' she paused, it seemed for some kind of applause, but none came, ' . . . there is a charity called the Actors' Fund. Don't you think it would be totally cute to be helping raise money for something we might actually need to dip into one day?'

'Dip into . . . Miss Wright?' Mrs Spittleforth queried over her spectacles.

'I mean, every actor might be outta work one of these days . . . wouldn't it be cool to fundraise for a charity which is actually relevant to our lives, rather than helping some community in Africa build a school we'll never ever get to go to?' Lavinia continued.

I know, Story-seeker . . . is this girl for real? She really thinks that what she's saying makes perfect sense.

'I don't think that's right, actually,' piped up Alice Parks. 'My dad said everyone who needs help, deserves help; it doesn't matter whether they live in your home, up the road, or on the other side of the world. That's what charity means.'

'Exact-ly! Bravissima, Alice!' Sofia said.

Lavinia looked at Lucinda for back-up, but she was

♥ *39* ♥

still seething about Maria's earlier outburst and too busy plotting against the Fitzfoster twins to notice.

Suddenly Molly stood up. 'I've got a story to tell you, which has become very personal to me. In fact, I can't think about anything else at the moment.'

'Finally!' said Daisy, the bassoonist. 'Someone with a bit of sense!'

As Molly told the girls the story of how she had met Calum huddled in a London doorway and described how badly he was being treated by the world around him (she couldn't face mentioning the Marciano car soaking him from head to toe), she could see the emotion in her friends' faces.

'Honestly, all of you, if we don't do something to help, I fear Maria, Sally and I aren't going to get any sleep this term,' Pippa joked, making Sally smile, just hearing her name mentioned as part of their gang.

Molly looked desperate. 'Here's our chance to give him, and others like him, another chance, places they can go for a hot meal and a warm bed for the night. Come on, girls, what do you say? I think I'll burst with guilt if we don't do something to help,' she pleaded.

'You make a very good case, Molly,' Mrs Spittleforth said. 'Does anyone else have anything to rival our two suggested charities?' She paused for a response. 'No? Well, it seems fair to me then that we have the actors' charity from 1 Beta and the homeless charity from 1 Alpha. Two very worthy causes I'm sure. Shall we put it to the vote?' she asked, diplomatically. 'Everyone in favour of Lavinia's fund, hands up . . . ' Only two hands shot in the air.

'Thank you, Miss Wright and Miss Marciano. Am I to conclude then that the rest of you are in favour of the homeless charity?'

There was an immediate show of hands from the rest of the room.

'Lovely. That's the first part settled then.'

Lavinia had now gone the exact same shade of puce as Lucinda.

'So now to the fundraising event itself . . . yes, Charlotte?' said Mrs Spittleforth.

'I've been thinking about this since Madame Ruby mentioned it this morning. What about some sort of sponsored singathon? Not sure how it would work or anything yet, but something along the lines of the longest continuous singing of a song.' But as she was met with a few doubtful looks, Charlotte wondered herself whether this was such a good idea now that she said it out loud. 'OK, OK, you might be right. It would no doubt get boring singing the same song over and over again anyway.'

'Might get a sore throat too, Lottie, and ruin our voices before exam time,' Sofia said, concerned.

'How about a fashion show?' said Faye. 'We could get everyone to come up with an outfit design, I'll make them and we can sell tickets to friends and family.'

'That's a great idea, Faye, except it'll be you locked away in a room for days doing all the work. None of us has a clue when it comes to sewing,' said Nancy. Faye nodded. Nancy was right. What was she thinking! The nightmare of sewing all the costumes for the Christmas Gala at the end of the first term suddenly came flooding back and she shuddered.

'Fair point, Nancy.'

The girls sat thoughtfully for a moment.

'Er . . . I . . . I might have an idea,' Sally said quietly, her eyes firmly on her shoes.

'That'll be the day!' Lucinda spat nastily.

Maria gave her another evil look. 'Go on, Sally,' she said.

'Well, I was watching this film once, and they had an auction, and all the money raised went to charity. They had such fantastic prizes, which had been donated for free, they made a fortune. I'm sure we could pull in some pretty great prizes with a bit of help from our families and friends. Even if we only donate one thing each, that's twenty-one prizes, which is more than enough.' Sally finally dared to look up, and was met with the biggest round of applause!

'Sally, that's brilliant!' Molly said, jumping up and hugging her – quite forgetting to keep her cool around Lucinda and Lavinia.

'Perfect, Sally!' Alice agreed. 'I could get Dad to offer free parking at any of his car parks for a whole year.'

'Great, Alice!' Pippa said, grabbing a pen. 'Let's get these down on paper before we forget!'

'I'm sure we could get Daddy to donate a piece of jewellery,' Maria said. 'Put us down for a diamond, Pips.'

'My family has a hotel in Barbados,' Lara announced. 'I know we'll be able to get a free holiday. Not sure about flights though.'

'I can maybe help with flights. Mum's PA to the Chairman of British Airways. I reckon she might be able to pull something out of the bag,' Elizabeth said. 'We could run our two items as one super-prize, Lara. What do you think?'

'Girls, this is simply marvellous. See how quickly a plan comes together when you work as a team,' Mrs Spittleforth interrupted them. 'You'll need to speak with your families and confirm the prize options as soon as possible, then I'll report in to Madame Ruby and find out whether it would be possible to host the auction at L'Etoile before the term ends. I hope you're all prepared to be waitresses for the evening. The more contented your guests are, the more pennies they'll spend!'

'Me, a waitress? Dream on!' said Lavinia to Lucinda.

'And we'll need some entertainment and of course someone to host the auction. Pippa, perhaps you could co-ordinate some sort of performance for the evening. And Sally – perhaps you would compere the whole event, seeing as it was your idea.'

While Pippa blushed and nodded, Sally gasped. 'Me? In front of all those people . . . I couldn't poss—'

'Absolutely she couldn't!' Lucinda jumped up. 'With my own and Lavinia's performance experience, it's obvious that *we* should host the evening as a double act. The rest of you will be busy serving supper.'

Just as Maria was getting ready to rugby-tackle Lucinda, Mrs Spittleforth surprised them all.

'Actually Miss Marciano, Miss Wright, I don't believe I heard Sally's response to my question . . . Miss Sudbury. I seem to remember, from the poem you wrote for the gala, that you have a gift for writing, so as long as you work on a good script, I think you would make a fine compere. How would you feel about taking on such a task? It would be quite the adventure I should imagine.'

Sally thought her legs might give way. She'd asked Maria for an adventure, and she seemed to have been granted her wish!

'Go on, Sal,' Pippa urged.

'Say yes, Sally,' Molly joined in. 'We'll help you every step of the way.'

'Er, I think . . . I think . . . yes please,' Sally finally answered and the girls clapped and cheered.

'Don't think being the hostess gets you out of donating a prize, Sudbury, the housekeeper's daughter. What are you going to donate? A pair of rubber gloves? A free spring clean?' Lucinda said.

'She'll be fine!' Pippa said bravely, mouthing at Sally to ignore her.

'Right, that's quite enough for this afternoon,' Miss Spittleforth concluded.

'Good work, girls. Pippa, seeing as you've kindly

been making notes, I would like to see a completed auction prize list in the next fortnight and jot down any other ideas you would like me to run past Madame Ruby.

'Class dismissed.'

6

The Penny Drops

That first day of term felt like the longest day on the planet. Sally was desperate to get out of classes where she wasn't being picked on by Lucinda and Lavinia, and Lucinda and Lavinia were even more desperate to get back to their room to finally have the chance to discuss the events of the day.

'I'm telling you, honey-pie, there is more to that Sally girl than you give her credit for,' Lavinia began, as soon as they closed their door. 'I thought you said she hated those geeks. It sure didn't look that way to me.'

'It's ridiculous; she detests them, as I do, especially that Pippa girl! Although those dumb Fitzfoster twins weren't on my hit-list until the brunette picked a fight with me today. She's now number one on the Marciano Revenge Radar,' Lucinda answered, throwing her satchel at the wall in anger.

'You're not listening to me, doll. You think butter wouldn't melt and that the housekeeper's kid is too stupid to play you, but you've got blinkers on where she's concerned,' Lavinia continued. 'Tell me again exactly what happened at that Christmas Gala. As I recall, you thought it was Pippa who dropped you in it. But I'm telling you, Sally is much too friendly with those girls. I totally think she was involved.'

'No way, L. There's no way that little weakling betrayed me. She wouldn't dare!'

'Well, I didn't see much evidence of fear today, Luci, when she took up the auction host role even though she knew you and I would be the best girls for the job.'

Lucinda sat thoughtfully for a moment until suddenly the penny started to drop. There had been far too many holes in what she'd thought might have happened on gala night. The biggest one was how Pippa had found out Lucinda was going to be miming her song, *Life's a Dream*, and knew to do a CD swap. As far as she remembered, she'd told Pippa she had just wanted to sing her song, not steal her voice. Oh my days, the only other person she'd trusted with the 'mime' aspect of the plot had been Sally!

'Lavinia, I hate to say it but I think you're right! Sally was nowhere to be seen on the night of the gala either – obviously keeping a low profile, knowing she'd betrayed me. I bet they've set this whole room-mate thing up! I've been so naive.' And then Lucinda did something she'd never done before. She burst into tears – for real!

Lavinia grabbed her arm roughly. 'No time for weakness here, Luci baby, only payback. So now you know about it . . . what are you going to do about it?'

'What am I *not* going to do about it?' Lucinda exploded, tears turning to rage. 'I'm going to hit Sudbury where it'll hurt the most and start with that mother of hers, that's what.'

Seconds later, Lucinda was on the phone to her father in LA, painting the blackest, meanest picture of Sally and the part she had played in the humiliation of the entire Marciano family at the Christmas Gala. Then she proceeded to criticise Sally's mother, the Marcianos' housekeeper. By the end of the call, Blue Marciano was already speed-dialling Maggie Sudbury to give her the immediate sack.

Lucinda hung up with a huge smirk on her face. She could cross one name off the Marciano Revenge Radar: ~~SALLY SUDBURY.~~

'Can you believe what happened today, Sally? You did say you wanted a bit of excitement – but this might be a bit more than you bargained for,' said Maria, smiling.

'Don't remind me. I only just about made it through a two-minute poem on stage at the Christmas Gala. How the flipping heck am I going to stand up in front of all those people for twenty-one auction items?' Sally answered, hugging her pillow to her chest.

Molly couldn't bear seeing her friend so vulnerable. 'Just you wait and see, Sally – by the time I've finished with you, you're going to look and feel a million dollars at that auction. You'll be desperate to get on that stage and show everyone in the place what you're made of.'

'Thanks, Molly. I don't mean to be pathetic, it's just I've never been given such a moment in the spotlight. What if I forget what prizes are on offer and muddle up who wins what? You know what a fluster I get into – and it'll be even worse knowing Luci and Lavi are just desperate for me to screw this up.'

'Would it help if Molly and I are your two assistants?' Maria suggested, secretly keen to do anything other than be a waitress serving supper. She and Molly had once asked their parents if they could help at one of the Fitzfoster summer parties, thinking it would be a bit of a laugh. While Molly had been the *hostess with the mostess*, Maria soon discovered she was hopeless at small talk and even worse at balancing plates up her arm like a proper silver-service waitress.

'What a good idea, Mimi,' said Molly. 'Once we know what prizes we've got, you could put together an auction list and get Dad's secretary to print a load of copies so that we can make sure there's one for every guest as part of their place setting.' She paused. 'In fact, scrap asking Dad. Mum's the queen of charity events. With all the fundraisers she's hosted over the years, I'm sure she's already got templates for this kind of thing and would know the cheapest place to get programmes printed. Maria, why not email her about it tonight and see if she's got any other ideas.'

'Yes, boss!' Maria mocked, but Molly was so busy making plans, she was oblivious to her sister's sarcastic response.

'And would you email Dad while you're at it? We

need to see if he can donate a Fitzfoster diamond.'

'And just what are you going to be doing for the next hour, while I'm being your personal assistant?' Maria asked, exasperated.

'I am going to be Miss Sally's personal stylist and beauty therapist!'

'You are?' Sally squealed with delight. She'd watched Molly work her makeover magic on most of the first years since they'd joined L'Etoile but never imagined she'd get the opportunity to experience it.

'And you're going to help me, Pippa,' Molly continued. 'Until now, you've been my pride and joy in terms of a makeover success story, but I've a feeling Sally is going to knock you off the top spot!'

'Charming!' Pippa grinned, but she knew Molly was trying to boost Sally's confidence, just as she'd helped her to feel like a goddess last Christmas.

As Molly got to work on Sally, Pippa was wracking her brains about what she might be able to donate to the auction. She felt a bit under pressure to come up with something fabulous like the other girls, but her family didn't own a hotel in Barbados last time she checked, so she was trying to be a bit more creative.

'Girls, I've been thinking about my prize. How do you think a day in the studio with Uncle Harry, writing and recording a track, would go down with our guests?'

'That's a brilliant idea, Pippa,' Molly said, a hairpin between her teeth. 'Especially if you were there too to lend a songwriting hand! There's nobody better.'

'Thanks!' Pippa continued. 'I can't expect anyone to pay a fortune to record in Uncle Harry's makeshift garden studio, though. It's fine for us, but it's hardly the rock-and-roll experience I'd like to offer. Don't suppose any of you girls have a state-of-the-art music studio tucked up your sleeve, do you? It would be a brilliant prize if it offered a first-class recording experience. I think it'd be such blast for Uncle Harry too.'

'Not that I can think of, Pips,' Maria answered. 'But why don't you talk to Miss Hart about your vision? Maybe she can have a word with Mr Fuller. I'm sure he's got recording studios in his office building we could use. I bet he'll be only too happy to donate a day or two somewhere in connection with your offer of providing the best producer and songwriter duo in town! He might even pop in and check out the winner's track. It's for a good cause, after all!'

'Perfect!' Pippa grinned, feeling rather more excited about her auction idea now. 'Why didn't I think of that? I'll email Miss Hart right away. Maybe she'll get a chance to discuss it with him tonight, or over the weekend.'

'Any chance you girls can help me too?' Sally asked, struggling to see out past half a dozen pink Velcro curlers. 'I mean, if you have any ideas about something I can donate. I can't imagine the Marcianos will be very forthcoming with a prize for me to offer. Right now, Lucifette's joke about me donating a pair of rubber gloves is the only option I can think of.'

'Nonsense!' Maria said. 'Don't worry, Sally. We'll think of something great. And if Lucifette wants rubber gloves, we'll make sure they're diamond-encrusted! That would shut them up, wouldn't it?' she said, chuckling.

'Molly, this is beyond a joke . . . I'm shattered! Haven't you finished with Sally yet?' Maria groaned. It had been about two hours since Molly had started Sally's makeover and everyone had had enough – not least Sally, who was frantic to see the final result.

'I know, I know. CO, Mimi.

CO = chill out, Story-seeker.

Just one more stroke of *Glimmerglass* lipgloss . . . there! Done!' As Molly swivelled Sally's chair around to face the mirror, Sally gasped so hard she nearly choked.

'Tah dah!' Molly sang.

'Oh, Molly! I can't believe it's me. How did you . . . ? What did you . . . ?' she asked, turning her head from side to side to try and see the back of her head where Molly had twisted and tousled every strand into a relaxed up-do.

'Sally, you look like the real you! Just the enhanced super-glamorous you!'

'You can say that again. Oh, Molly, thank you so much. I feel fantastic. It's so weird, it's as if a weight has been lifted from my shoulders. I always feel so dowdy, but looking like this, I feel I could take on the world single-handed.'

'Blimey, Molly. What's in that hairspray? I think I need some,' Maria giggled.

Molly gave Maria her best *shut-up-sis-or-else* look.

'I'm just so relieved you're happy. I never know how a person's going to react to my styling. How you look is so personal and there is nothing worse in life than having a *bad hair day,*' she continued, deadly serious.

'Thank you, Molly, for everything. I can't explain how wonderful it is to finally feel part of something.'

'Ahhhh, no one deserves friendship more, Sal. Friends forever?' Pippa asked with a wink.

'Friends forever!' the twins and Sally chanted Pippa's own song lyric back at her.

'Forever might come to an end sooner than you think if we don't get to bed and turn these lights off. Miss Coates will come down on us like a ton of bricks if we're caught chatting instead of snoring,' Maria said, absolutely exhausted.

She'd spent the earlier part of the evening locked in discussions with Madame Ruby and Miss Hart about the student tours at the weekend.

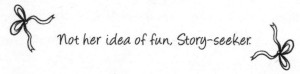

Not her idea of fun, Story-seeker.

'You're right,' said Sally. 'But not before you've got a few pics of me looking like this! I'm desperate to send them to Mum.'

Maria smiled as she watched the new, confident Sally strike pose after pose while Molly snapped away with her camera. What a difference a *Mollywood makeover* makes!

'Thanks, Moll. Those photos are fantastic. At least

when I wake up, I'll know it wasn't all a dream,' Sally said as she dived under her duvet.

'Hang on a sec, Miss Sally! Aren't you going to put your pyjamas on?' Molly asked.

'Don't think they'll go with the hair and make-up, do you? And I'm nowhere near ready to remove my new princess look yet. I've only just got it! Night, y'all!' Sally said, switching off the last lamp.

'Night, *Princess Sally*,' Pippa said. And with that, the four room-mates fell into a deep slumber.

7

Fighting Fire with Fire

'I can't take much more of this,' Maria said as she flung her satchel on her bed from the door of their room.

'Where have you been this time, Mimi? You just seemed to disappear after supper,' said Molly.

'I know – I didn't even get the chance to tell you I was going anywhere. Madame Ruby grabbed me in the Ivy Room saying she just wanted to run through the Lost Rose tour one last time so that everything runs smoothly this weekend for the student mini-tours. Honestly – it's fine – but she's got her knickers in a complete twist about it!

'They've asked three of the best sixth-form actresses

– Lucy Foster, Maya Chandler and Fearne Holmes –
to pretend to be us three treasure-hunting L'Etoilettes,
and then guests will be split into groups of twenty and
guided on their own hunt for the Lost Rose using
replicas of Frank's clues, starting as we did below the
gold star door-knocker.'

'Sounds wonderful. Everyone must be so excited.
And Mimi, it just goes to show, they'd be lost without
you. I bet you can't wait to start bossing those sixth-
formers about!' Molly said, giving her sister a squeeze.
'Just one more weekend to get through, then you can
hand it over.'

'I don't know what you mean!' Maria winked,
loving the idea of being in charge. 'I've made a couple
of suggestions . . . the first one being that they should
have understudies for Lucy, Maya and Fearne. Can't
believe they hadn't thought of that. Now they're
having a whole team of "us" to rotate the roles over
the summer. Makes much more sense!'

'Ever the genius, sis!' Molly said, grinning, and
knowing the sixth form had no idea what they were
in for that weekend. 'Perhaps the mysterious *Yours,
L'Etoilette* should file her first blog of the summer
term on Sunday night, reporting back on how the
tours went.'

'Oh yes!' Pippa joined in. 'I've missed her humour. You could even get her to interview *you*, Maria, so that you can give a proper account of the tours without it looking weird.'

'Great idea, Pippa. I'll do just that. I was wondering what to kick the term off with and that's perfect. It'll be a great way to get some feedback on the tours from the girls too,' she answered, her mind already buzzing with catchy headlines.

'Sally!' Molly exploded, as Sally's tear-stained face appeared in the doorway. 'What's happened?'

'I-i-i-i-t's Mum,' she sobbed into her sleeve. 'You w-w-w-on't b-b-believe what she's done.'

'What's your mum done? What do you mean?' Pippa asked.

'No, not what M-M-Mum's done,' Sally stammered, tears rolling down her cheeks. 'What she's done to Mum – L-L-Lucifette.' She took a couple of deep breaths, worried that she was never going to get her story out. 'I-I-I think the penny must have finally dropped yesterday at the charity discussion with old Butter-boots,' she began. 'With Lucifette, I mean. It looks like she and Lavinia have realised that we're best friends and that being sent to share a room with you isn't the punishment they thought it would be.'

'I had a feeling something like this would happen, if I'm honest,' Maria said. 'I put us on Lucifette's radar when I stood up for Belle – and then we all supported you about hosting the auction. I could see the cogs in Lavatory's brain whirring, working out exactly what we are all about. I think she's the one who's stirred this up. Lucifette wouldn't have the brains on her own.'

'Blimey, do you think they've worked out that Sally had something to do with the Christmas Gala exposé too, then?' asked Pippa, watching Sally's eyes widen with fear.

'I hadn't thought of that, but now you mention it, I reckon they definitely know it was me. Lucifette wouldn't have been quite this spiteful otherwise. She's been so evil this time,' Sally paused, staring at her three new best friends, who were hanging on her every word.

'Miss Hart sent for me with an urgent message to phone my mum. I could hardly make out what she was saying, she was crying so much. Basically, she's been given the sack and told that we have to get out of the housekeeper's cottage by the end of the week! I'm allowed to stay at L'Etoile until the end of the year as this term's fees have already been paid, but I'll have to pay after that, or leave!'

'That little witch!' Maria said. 'How can she be so nasty? I can just imagine the sorts of things she said to her parents. It's not fair. They're the ones who should be jobless, school-less and homeless, not you and your poor mum.'

Sally looked up red-eyed and weepy. 'She said she had the most hideous phone call from Mr Marciano, who accused her of being really unhygienic in the kitchen and hinted that items had been disappearing without explanation.' She burst into tears again. 'Mum is devastated. She's the most hard-working, *honest* person on the planet. She would *never* steal anything from anyone.'

'Of course she wouldn't,' Molly said. 'He made the whole thing up – or at least he was repeating the lies that Lucifette told him . . . ' Molly scrabbled around in the chocolate chest.

'Here, have one of these; they always make me feel better!' She handed Sally the most enormous tightly wound wheel of strawberry shoelace. 'In fact, desperate times call for desperate measures. Let's all have one,' she said, passing one to Pippa and Maria, but Maria was on her feet and halfway out of the door.

'Maria, where are you going now? Can't you sit here for two seconds while we try and sort this mess out for Sally? I can't bear her being so sad. There must be something we can do to help!' Molly exclaimed.

'Give me a minute. I need to make a phone call,' Maria said, disappearing into the corridor.

Sally had to admit the sugary strawberry sweetness did make her feel a bit better, but only for a few moments. As soon as it was finished, the despair she felt at the thought of losing her wonderful new friends opened the floodgates again and she buried her face in her tear-soaked pillow.

'Did someone use the words "genius" and "me" in the same sentence earlier?' Maria said with a big grin as she came back into their room. 'If they didn't, they should have done!'

Molly jumped up and hugged her sister. She had no idea what Maria had been up to but she knew her sister had a knack for fixing the *unfixable* and she was sure she had good news.

'What's ha-bbened?' Sally asked, her nose blocked up from crying.

'Well, it's Dad you need to thank really. I suddenly remembered a conversation I'd overheard at Easter. Even though we live in London most of the time, Mum and Dad also have a house in the country which we go to sometimes in the holidays as it has loads of lovely outside space for us to get up to no good. Can't wait for you girls to see it. It's awesome!'

'Mimi, get to the point, will you? What's Dad said?' Molly said, impatiently.

Daddy dear is, as we speak, on the phone to your mum, Sally, asking if she would consider being our new housekeeper at Wilton House. The conversation I overheard at Easter was between him and Susie, our country housekeeper, who'd said she would like to retire, but that she'd only do it when we'd found the right person to take over from her rather than leave us in the lurch. Can you believe it?' said Maria.

'I can't believe it,' Sally answered in shock.

'I know! WATC, Sal!' said Molly. 'And the best of it is, you'll obviously live in the gatehouse with your mum so you'll always be there to spend the whole summer with us. How brilliant is that?' She quickly turned to Pippa, aware she might feel left out. 'And, of course, there'll be a room with your name on it too, Pips, for whenever you want to come and stay with us this summer and every summer!'

'Aaaand . . . there's more . . . ' Maria announced. 'Dad said that if your mum's willing to work some weekends when we're all actually living at the house, then instead of paying her overtime, he'll take care of your school fees. That way, you get to stay here with us at L'Etoile. What about that for good news!' said Maria, feeling very pleased with herself.

'Oh my goodness!' Sally said.

'I don't know what to say, girls. THANK YOU!' She flung her arms around their necks. 'It's just too good to be true. I could never have imagined a better outcome. I'm finally free of that spiteful family. And so is Mum! She stuck with it all so that I could have the best things. Her proudest moment was seeing me on the stage at the Christmas Gala, reading my poem.'

'What?' Molly, Maria and Pippa all said at once.

'We didn't know your mum was there!' Molly said.

'I wasn't allowed to mention it – Mrs Marciano couldn't bear the fact that she had to take a member of the domestic staff to an event she was attending herself. She said Mum could come along if she got the train, watched from the back of the hall, and left before the theatre lights went up,' Sally explained.

'Cripes, that's awful!' Maria said. 'She's your mother!'

Sally tumbled backwards onto her bed, with the biggest smile on her face. 'What a day!'

'And I for one can't wait to tell Lucifette the good news!' said Maria with a glint in her eye.

'She'll hit the roof!' Sally said. 'But who cares . . . not my problem any more! Good riddance to bad Marciano rubbish I say!'

'Ha! That's the spirit,' Pippa giggled, also enjoying the feeling of being one up on Lucinda.

'Maria, could I ask one last favour and borrow your phone? I'm desperate to speak to Mum and see if she's spoken to your dad. I reckon she'll be in complete shock if she has, but happy!' said Sally.

'Of course!' Maria said, with a scowl as she spotted her sister *Mollifying* her beloved mobile with a thousand gold star-shaped crystals. 'Thank you for that, Molly . . . NOT!' she snapped, and then turned back to Sally. 'And just to add brilliance to genius, I was thinking, I'm sure Dad would let you offer a weekend at the house as your auction prize. You'd have to speak to your mum about the cooking and stuff for the prize-winners, and if she'd mind looking after them. I'm sure it'll get loads of bidders. Everyone loves a weekend in the country.'

Sally squeezed Maria's hand as hard as she dared without hurting her and ran off to phone her mum. How could she ever repay the Fitzfoster kindness? She'd have to think of a way.

Knock knock.

'Sally, you don't have to knock, darling. You live here!' Molly called as she opened the door.

'Belle! Sorry, thought you'd be Sally. She's just nipped out to make a phone call.'

'Yes, I saw her on the way up. She's in floods of tears, but smiling so I didn't think I needed to check if she was all right,' Belle said, wondering what was going on.

'Ah, she's fine, Belle. Don't worry,' said Pippa. 'Just some family stuff but it's sorted now.'

'What can we do for you, Miss Brown?' Molly asked.

'There are two things. First — Maria, I wanted to thank you for sticking up for me with Lucifette.

I can't tell you how petrified I am of that girl. I couldn't believe my bad luck when she picked on me. I wouldn't have dared correct her. She's always called me Bill. How insulting is that?' said Belle.

'My pleasure!' Maria said boldly. 'And you can spread the word that we're not taking any more of Luci and Lavi's rubbish. I'm not having them think they can bully whoever they fancy. It's just not on!'

'I think you're really brave. I'm going to try to be a bit stronger, Maria, to support you,' Belle promised. 'The next thing I wanted to talk to you about – as you're in charge of the auction list, Pippa – is an idea for a souvenir for the evening. My family own a toy factory and I was thinking, what if they made up a batch of fluffy black Labrador "Twinkle" puppies to sell on the evening as an extra money-spinner. What do you think?'

'Belle, that's a brilliant idea!' Molly exclaimed. 'How clever of you! I can't imagine a single guest not buying one for their daughter. They'd be sooo cute. Every girl needs a Twinkle guard dog to watch over them while they sleep.'

'I've been wracking my brains about something for my family to donate and it suddenly came to me when

I spotted Twinkle running round the quad with Mr Hart this afternoon,' Belle said.

'I wonder whether instead of the usual metal name disc on a dog collar, it could be a little glass ruby – a Lost Rose replica,' Molly wondered out loud.

'Yes! Fantabulous idea, Moll!' Maria exclaimed, another plan forming in her busy mind. 'Don't you see? If we tie it in with the Legend of the Lost Rose, we might be able to sell the fluffy Twinkles as souvenirs during the summer mystery tours. Madame Ruby couldn't refuse. That way, there would be a constant stream of money coming in for our charity, way beyond the auction.'

'Now that's what I call a plan!' Belle exclaimed. 'I'll have to speak to Mum and Dad and see what the schedules are and whether they can cope with the additional production line throughout the summer. Can't see why it would be a problem, though. The only thing is that they'd obviously donate the toys free for the auction night, but they'll need to cover their production costs for the summer tour sales. I don't think it would be much and there will still be a huge profit for the tours. Right then, I'll see you tomorrow, L'Etoilettes! And thanks again, Maria.'

As Belle left, Sally came back from talking to her

mum, who was thrilled at the prospect of a fresh start and not having to worry about her daughter's future.

After Molly had finished filling her in on the fluffy Twinkle plan, she sat down on the bed and sighed a happy sigh.

'Wow, girls! What a productive evening we've had. That's two amazing ideas in the last hour. Imagine what we'd be able to solve in a week if we didn't have to do school work! Four heads are most definitely better than one. This is shaping up to be a fantastic term!'

8

The Battle Continues

$\mathcal{L}$ucinda's and Lavinia's smug faces were almost unbearable to look at the following day.

'I'm really sorry to hear about your mum's job,' Betsy said to Sally in the lunch queue.

Sally couldn't believe her ears. 'What did you say, Betsy?'

'I said, I'm sorry to hear about your mum losing her job. That must be tough. Can't imagine you'll be too sad about leaving that household, though, will you?'

Who could have been talking about her business? It wouldn't have been the twins or Pippa. And Lucinda couldn't possibly be bragging to everyone about leaving her and her mother homeless, could she? Suddenly, her ears picked up on a conversation Lucinda was having with Amanda Lloyd.

'I mean . . . you can't get the staff . . . stealing from under our noses like that . . . Pop had no choice . . .'

Sally was fuming. That did it! If that horror-hog couldn't keep her mouth shut, then why should she? She grabbed her first opportunity.

'Oh, thank you, Betsy, that's kind of you, but Mum and I are absolutely fine about leaving the Marciano household. It's always been a bit of a nightmare, to be honest. And, as luck would have it, we are on to bigger and better things. In fact it's no secret that Molly and Maria's father has already employed Mum to run the Fitzfosters' country house. It's so exciting. And I'll be staying at L'Etoile, which means I'll never have to leave my new best girls. It's all rather fabulous.'

Sally couldn't believe that she had the nerve to be so gushing, and so loudly at that.

Lavinia, who happened to be passing Sally in time to hear the words *Maria's father has already employed Mum*, hovered to listen to the rest of the conversation. Seeing red, she deliberately slammed into Sally's side, tipping a lunch tray of stinky beef stew and blackberry crumble all over her uniform.

'I saw that, Lavinia Wright!' Maria shouted, bolting over to Sally's side.

Totally ignoring Maria's accusation, Lavinia began flailing her arms and apologising loudly, insisting the whole thing had been an accident. So far the only person to run to her aid was Lucinda, but she kept very quiet.

'Why you devious, spiteful, stuck-up little weasel!' Maria continued, angrier than Molly had ever seen her. And the more Lavinia ignored her, the more furious Maria became. Suddenly, without even thinking about the consequences, Maria scooped a handful of blackberry crumble from Elizabeth's plate and threw it at Lavinia. She stood, in total shock, purple juice dripping down her right cheek into a sticky puddle on her shoulder.

As everyone started to giggle at how ridiculous Lavinia looked, Maria suddenly calmed down and couldn't believe what she'd done. Just as Lavinia was about to repeat the act by grabbing a fistful of soggy creamed spinach to launch at Maria, she suddenly spied Mackle the Jackal, making a beeline for the disturbance.

'What is going on in my dining room?' Mackle boomed at the pair of them.

Before Maria could explain – although there would have had to be some pretty fancy explaining to get herself off this hook – Lavinia had already taken centre stage, painting herself as the victim, complete with crocodile tears and wailing about being bullied. Old Mackle didn't even give Maria a chance to have her say before she sent her directly to Madame Ruby's office to explain her behaviour.

If the truth be known, Story-seeker, Mackle the Jackal couldn't believe her luck when she saw who was at the centre of this latest dining-room disaster. Those twins had tricked her before, she was sure of it, but she wasn't about to let them get away with it a second time. Ever since that day, she'd not been able to scold any student for their leftovers. It had been clean plate after clean plate at the tray clearing station. At last she'd had her revenge, small and petty as it was!

Luci had dragged Lavi straight to their room for an urgent debrief following L'Etoile's first ever food fight.

'What happened, Lavinia?' Lucinda asked in

earnest. 'One minute I was talking to Amanda, waiting for you and next thing Sudbury is standing there covered in your lunch and then one of the Fitzfoster losers is flinging her crumble over you!'

'I just saw red,' Lavinia said, still shaky. Believe me, you'd have done the same if you'd overheard what I overheard, Luci.'

'What are you talking about?' Lucinda asked.

'I can't believe you still don't know. That Fitzfoster family has only gone and hired Sally's mum, so they're fine – all sorted as far as I can tell – and to top it off, and I quote, Sally gets to be with her "*new best friends always*" – unquote,' Lavinia said, impersonating Sally.

'WHAT?' Lucinda exploded. 'Impossible! Pop would never have given her a reference.'

'I don't think she needed one with them! Bunch of do-gooders!' answered Lavinia.

'I can't believe it. Just when we think we've got one over on them, they do this! What can we do next, L? We can't let them think they've won!' Lucinda fumed.

'There is something, but it's huge and will get at least one of them expelled!' Lavinia said, licking her lips like a cat about to pounce. 'Are you in?'

'You bet I'm in. If one goes, hopefully they'll all follow. If we target Maria, that pathetic twin Molly will never stay at L'Etoile without her, and I'm guessing the family will send Sally wherever the girls go. That'll just leave Pippa – but if she's alone, we can make it our business to make her wish she'd never taken up that scholarship. Bring it on, L, I'm all ears, sweetie!'

Lavinia nodded and took a deep breath. This was going to be pretty shocking, even by her standards.

'First I need to tell you a secret,' Lavinia began. 'I haven't told you before as I was sworn to secrecy – not sure why – but there you go. OK. Once Mom knew I was coming to L'Etoile, she got in touch with Madame Ruby to see if she could bring her whole show over and make a forty-eight-hour fly-on-the-wall documentary about this world-famous British School for Stars . . .'

'Amazing!' Lucinda interrupted. 'Sorry! Carry on . . . I shan't say another word until you're done.'

'The whole thing's a ploy to boost L'Etoile's presence in America and to raise Mom's profile in the UK. Anyway, they're going to come the week of the exams so there are plenty of live performances for them to film, but then, for the first years only, obviously all thanks to *me*, Mom's going to hold a talk-show workshop where she'll conduct live interviews with staff and students, to give everyone an insight into how she became the world's greatest chat-show host.'

'Wow!' Lucinda could have kicked herself for butting in again. 'Sorry, L!'

'And this, Luci honey, is where we put a spin on things and make this the best show Mom's ever recorded! It's going to take some thinking about, but here's my idea.' She took another breath. 'What if we were to set one of those girls up – like frame them for stealing exam papers right before the exams – and somehow manipulate the film crew and my mom into revealing the cheats during filming. No one would be able to deny it had happened or wasn't real and Madame Ruby would have no alternative but to expel them – all on camera! How's that for a master plan?!'

Lucinda would never have admitted it, but total annihilation of the career of another student wasn't quite as far as she would have taken it herself, but who was she to criticise Lavinia? There was no denying that the plan was quite brilliant! And she'd thought *she* was devious. She had nothing on Lavinia Wright! This was a whole new level of nasty!

'I love it, Lavinia! You're a genius!' Lucinda cooed, so pleased to have this girl on her side.

'Like I said, it's going to take some planning. I think

first we need to do some research on which member of staff is the exam coordinator and where they keep the exam papers. We'll have to bide our time until a night or two before the exams to be sure the papers have all been written. At my last school, I remember most of the tutors handing in their documents the night before so that they covered everything, up to and including that day's lessons.'

'Yes, and then we'll have to work out the best time to sneak them into the twins' room so that they can be found easily by the film crew, but not so early that the twins spot them before we're ready,' said Lucinda, thoughtfully.

'Exactly!' answered Lavinia. 'Come on then, we've no time to lose!'

9

There's Good News and Bad News

Maria sat outside Madame Ruby's office, waiting to be called in to hear her fate. She'd resigned herself to whatever punishment was coming her way. Despite having had what she felt were very noble reasons for acting as she did, she had to agree that there was no excuse for throwing food at another student. It was childish and she was so cross with herself for using fists to convey her emotions, rather than her brain. She vowed then and there never to lose her cool like that again.

Still, nobody's perfect all the time — yes, not even Maria, Story-seeker.

After a few minutes, she realised that Madame Ruby was actually on the phone, so Maria thought she'd take the opportunity to check her emails on her mobile – breaking more L'Etoile rules. She could hardly believe her eyes! There was only one unread email in her inbox and it was from her heroine, the *London Gazette* journalist who'd indirectly helped her solve the Legend of the Lost Rose, Luscious Tangerella. Maria could hear her heart beating as she opened the email and read:

From: luscious.tangerella@londongazette.co.uk
To: maria.fitzfoster@letoile.co.uk
Date:14th May
Subject: Is this of interest?
📎: Gazelle competition.pdf

Hello Maria,
I hope you are well and that you and your family and friends enjoyed the piece in *Gazelle* over Easter. It was one of those stories that I felt particularly proud to be involved with so thank you again for granting me the exclusive.

I'm sure you're deeply ensconced with exams but just wanted to let you know about a competition my editor is running for budding young journalists. Applicants are to write a 3,000-word article on a subject of their choice and I really think you should enter. The entry deadline isn't until the end of term so you'll have plenty of time to think about it and write, without it interrupting your studies. First prize sees the winner's article appear in *Gazelle* and offers a week's work experience shadowing the nation's favourite columnist – yours truly ;-)

Anyway – it's totally up to you, Maria. I've attached an entry form, if you are interested.

Good luck!
Yours,
Luscious T x

Maria was so busy reading and re-reading the email that she hadn't noticed Madame Ruby standing in the doorway of her office, impatiently tapping her fingers.

'Hem . . . Hem . . . Miss Fitzfoster. I would have thought you would have already had quite enough of my office for this term.'

Maria jumped so hard, her phone slipped out of her fingers and clattered to the floor, finally resting in a puddle of Molly's gold stars.

Madame Ruby rolled her eyes. If students were as stupid as to be breaking the rules on her very doorstep, she was at a complete loss for words.

'Let's get this over with, shall we?' she said and motioned to Maria to follow her in.

Maria began to explain what happened in the Ivy Room, only to be met by Madame Ruby flinging up her hand in a *stop now* fashion.

'I don't understand, Madame,' Maria said, confused. 'I'm here to explain my actions and receive my punishment.'

'Is that so?' Madame Ruby answered, seeming to find something amusing. 'To be honest, Maria, of all my students, you are the least likely candidate I would expect to find guilty of such petty nonsense. In fact I don't even wish to hear any more. I suggest you go away and have a good think about your ridiculous actions, and if there is a next time, I will come down on you like a ton of bricks for pure stupidity . . . which for you, would be quite a name tag!'

'Yes, Madame, thank you,' Maria murmured in disbelief.

The headmistress looked deadly serious for a moment. 'Maria,' she said. 'I mean that. I won't be lenient a second time.'

'Absolutely, Madame. Understood,' Maria answered.

'Now is there anything else? Or can I get back to more pressing issues?'

'Well, actually, yes there is, Madame Ruby. If I may show you an email I've just received from Luscious Tangerella.'

Madame Ruby's ears pricked up. She loved a bit of showbiz. 'This is more like it, Maria. Show me immediately.'

'Apologies, but the email is on my phone, Madame. You see it had only just come through when I was waiting outside your office. When you read it, hopefully you'll see why I was so distracted. I'd really like your approval and advice if possible,' and Maria handed her phone over.

Madame Ruby seemed to struggle with scrolling down to the bottom of the note on Maria's small phone, but eventually she said, 'This is wonderful, Maria. Of course you must enter the competition. In fact, consider the extra workload your punishment for today. Just one thing, though: I'd like to cast my eyes over the article before you send it back to Miss Tangerella, if you don't mind. Good luck, Maria. You may close the door behind you.'

'What? That's all she said?' Molly asked after Maria had told the girls about her meeting with old Ruby.

Wow! She is mellowing in her old age. It's ever since the Lost Rose appeared! It's as though it's cast some sort of spell over her,' said Pippa.

'It's weird, isn't it? She's not the old bat we thought – either that or she's just reeling us in so she can keep a closer eye on us! That wouldn't surprise me either,' Maria said, suspiciously. 'Anyway, never mind old Ruby, any ideas on subject matter for this *Gazette* competition. I can't think of anything that is going to help me stand out from the crowd.'

'You'll think of something special, I just know it, Mimi,' Molly said. 'Luscious T must think you're in with a chance if she's taken the time to *ask* you to enter. I bet you feel all warm inside. It's high praise indeed!'

'I second that. Well done, Maria. Have you emailed her back yet? If not, you should, and as soon as possible. Don't want her thinking you lack efficiency!' said Pippa.

A look of panic flashed across Maria's face. The last thing she wanted to do was make a bad impression.

'CO, Pips. I think it's much more important that Maria takes her time to compose a reply tonight rather than rushing a response off now. Every word counts,' Molly said.

'Moll's right, I think,' said Sally. 'And regarding what subject you're going to choose for your article, I always think the simplest ideas are the best. Don't try to be too clever or too random. It's better to write about something you know, something close to your heart.' And as she was talking, an idea hit her. 'I've got it!' Sally exclaimed. 'You should do a diary – your diary – our diary – *The Secret Diary of a L'Etoilette*, and include all the highs and lows from your first year at the famous School for Stars. The *Gazette* will obviously have to know the entry has come from you – but you can write under an anonymous name like A. Star or something. It would give it a real air of mystery – and let's face it, you're the queen of mysteries, Maria – or solving them at least!'

'Sally, you're a genius! Reckon you should be the one to enter this competition. You'd walk it!' Maria replied.

'Ha! It's always much easier thinking of something when it's not for you,' Sally answered.

'I'll do it! It's perfect. What a weight off my mind. I might just shoot Madame Ruby a quick email to check she's happy with that subject matter. No doubt she'll have a few rules for me to stick to of things I can and can't mention but there shouldn't be too many restrictions. Then I can email Luscious T properly tonight! I might even interview *Yours, L'Etoilette* for the article – just as another L'Etoile mystery!'

'Girls, you'll forgive the interruption, but I have some important exam information,' Miss Hart announced, having gatecrashed 1 Alpha's technology lesson that afternoon.

'There will be three consecutive days set aside for your examinations. Examination day one will be next Wednesday, as you know, which will be for your practical artistic assessments. You should have already discussed this with your tutors and been given a time for your individual performances with the relevant tutor.'

Miss Hart paused to look around the room and was relieved to see everyone nodding in agreement.

'Marvellous. Exam day two will come as a bit of a surprise to you – and a good one I hope! I'm delighted to say that Madame Ruby received a request from our newest student's mother, the famous talk-show host Tallulah Wright, to bring a camera crew to L'Etoile. Mrs Wright has asked to host a talk-show workshop for the first-year students where she will conduct live interviews with staff and students to give you an insight into a career on television and how to get there. The show will be edited and televised both here and in America, which will be great exposure for you girls and raise the profile of L'Etoile in America.'

She paused again, slightly confused as to why the faces looking up at her were absolutely terrified.

'It's nothing to worry about, girls. You'll learn a tremendous amount about the world of television and how a show is put together from a woman who is one of the best, if not *the* best chat-show host in the world. Lastly, following the workshop, you will all receive a grade agreed by Mrs Wright and me, which will form part of your overall end-of-year mark. Any questions?'

No one said a word.

'Fine. Then that just leaves exam day three, which some of you may find a little daunting, given that it's back-to-back testing of the academic curriculum. L'Etoile tests its students slightly differently from most schools. We prefer to condense the academic testing into one full day, but each subject examination will only last for half an hour. We feel that intensive, quick-fire testing is far more beneficial and demonstrative of true learning levels than sitting students down for hours on end. I hope that provides some comfort to you all?'

No response.

'All right then. Thank you, girls, for your time. Mr West, apologies for taking up so much of your lesson. I'm off to see 1 Beta in the Einstein Quarter. Please do continue.'

No sooner had the bell sounded than Sally's panicked face appeared in the doorway of the computer room.

'Blimey, Sally. Did you even go to maths? How did you get here so quickly?' Pippa asked, picturing Sally bombing across the quad.

'Girls! So glad I caught you. Have you heard the news – about the horror-hog's mother and this hideous workshop?'

'Yes!' Lydia, Daisy and Alice said in unison, joining in the conversation.

'If the mother's anything like the daughter, we're in for trouble!' Pippa agreed, rolling her eyes.

'You have no idea,' Sally groaned.

'Oh, Sally. Come on, how bad can Tallulah Wright be for one day?' Maria asked, trying to make a little light of the situation.

'B-A-D,' Sally spelled out, her voice full of doom.

No one said any more on the subject. They were too busy dreading whether they'd be picked on and wondering how bad B-A-D was! Only time would tell!

10

Hide and Cheat

The weekend passed in a blur of the usual gossip and not-so-usual revising. The first years were beside themselves with exam worries. Every single music room, study room, classroom, even cloakroom was permanently occupied by a student practising for their individual performance exams on Wednesday. Then there was the dreaded exam day three on Friday – all the academic stuff.

There was only one person who wasn't bothered by that prospect – and yes, you've guessed, Story-seeker – Miss Maria. She didn't even need to swot up, much to the frustration of everyone around her. To be fair to

Maria, though, she'd still spent the weekend studying hard with the rest of the girls — just as a teacher rather than as a student. Pippa, Sally and Molly had never been so well-tutored!

By Monday morning, L'Etoile was teeming with engineers installing mini-cameras all over the school. In addition to the filming on Wednesday and Thursday, there would be some fly-on-the-wall type footage taken throughout the day on Tuesday. TW — Tallulah Wright — was hoping the girls would forget the cameras were there and do something topical that she could use as a talking point during her workshop on Thursday.

'Are you absolutely sure about this, L?' Lucinda asked her partner in crime as they ducked out of the Ivy Room early Monday evening and doubled back to the main school building.

'Absolutely positive, L. Mom's TV cameras won't be active until she arrives tomorrow. I've been hanging around outside the staffroom for the past week to find out how we can get our hands on those papers and I've seen the same red leather box file being carried about at different points by different teachers, but each time, it gets passed back to old Butter-boots. She's definitely responsible for it.'

'I just can't believe Madame Ruby would have trusted that scatterbrain to be the exam secretary. It's only a matter of time before she loses that exam file, with or without our help!' Lucinda whispered nastily, as they made their way along the corridor. 'Are you sure she's still in there? How do you know she didn't leave to go home already?'

'What is this – twenty questions?!' Lavinia exploded. 'You're going to have to trust me! I know because her yellow Beetle is still in the car park – look!'

By this point, Lucinda and Lavinia had positioned their naughty selves behind one of the huge sash window curtains next to the staffroom. Lucinda couldn't believe how much Lavinia had achieved in such a short time at L'Etoile. As she turned to the left slightly, she saw Audrey Butter's unmistakable buttercup-coloured VW parked in her space. Wow, Lavinia was good at being bad!

'Shhhh. Someone's coming!' Lavinia whispered. And lo and behold, no sooner had the staffroom door opened than old Butter-boots came trotting out, locking up behind her. Lucinda squeezed Lavinia's shoulder as she spied the red leather exam file, tucked under Mrs Butter's left arm. Lucinda was amazed.

It was as though their teacher was following a script Lavinia had written for her.

Audrey Butter walked down the corridor but stopped suddenly when she caught sight of her reflection in the enormous mirror above the hall-stand.

'Oh, my goodness gracious me. What do I look like?' she muttered to herself.

'This won't do at all. Marion won't forgive me if turn up looking like I've been dragged through a hedge backwards!'

Suddenly she threw her coat down and deposited the red box file, books and her handbag on the hall-stand and began rummaging around. 'Honestly, I think this school has Borrowers! I know I had a hairbrush in here this morn—' and then she stopped, remembering how she'd tossed it into her locker, along with a huge can of hairspray, that morning when she was running late for class. Still clutching her staffroom key, she looked at the red file and books on the hall-stand, glanced round to check no one was there – crazily said, 'Don't move! !' and marched back to the staffroom.

Lavinia could scarcely believe her luck. She hadn't expected it to be this easy. She'd hoped, at the very best, that the most they would achieve that evening would be to see where old Butter-boots locked the red file away at night. How could she have just left it unattended in the middle of the hall? If only she knew that the Borrowers were out in force tonight and intent on doing a lot worse than just *borrowing*!

As soon as they heard the door click shut, Lucinda watched in awe as her more devious and daring partner in crime raced over to the file, opened it, whipped out her phone, clicked photos of the front and back of the top exam paper, speedily replaced it, closed the file and was back at her side without so much as a swish of the curtain! Flippin' heck, this girl was good!

They held their breath as old Butter-boots reappeared in a haze of hairspray. She stopped again briefly to smooth the sides of her bird's-nest hair-do, gather her things and then scuttled down the corridor, muttering about how late she was going to be for Marion.

'I can't believe that all just happened so easily!' Lavinia gloated as she uploaded the photographs she'd taken of the exam paper. 'Can you believe she was so stupid? And, to be honest, she's lucky we just took pictures! Someone else might have taken the file and then the entire teaching staff would have had to start their exam prep from scratch!'

'Can you imagine? Poor old Butter-boots really would have been public enemy number one then,' Lucinda laughed, picturing Mrs Butter standing in Madame Ruby's office making excuses.

'Oh, wow,' Lavinia exclaimed as the first photo popped up onto her laptop screen. 'The ironic thing is that top paper is our history exam – old Butter-boots' own exam paper. She must have been finishing it off, right before we swooped!'

'You're joking. Let's have a look then. No point in letting this opportunity go to waste now we've got all the questions! I hate history. It'll make life so much easier knowing which answers to learn,' said Lucinda, grabbing the laptop from Lavinia and practically inhaling the words off the screen.

'When you've quite finished with that, Luci, I'm only going to print one copy and handle it with gloves on so there aren't any fingerprints. We can't be too careful. Last thing we want to do is get caught!' Lavinia said, sensibly.

'No chance, honey-pie. You were brilliant tonight. I couldn't have done a better job myself,' Lucinda praised her scheming friend.

'No, I noticed that!' Lavinia scoffed, slightly annoyed that so far, Lucinda hadn't done any of the dirty work. Come to think of it, she'd not even helped with the planning!

'Hmmm, what was that, L?' Lucinda muttered, still noting down the history topics to revise.

'Oh, never mind!' Lavinia snapped. Now wasn't the time for them to argue. They weren't out of the woods yet. They still had to figure out a way of getting the papers into the twins' bedroom without being seen, but they'd have a couple of days to think about that.

Before we move on, Story-seeker, we wanted to tell you a little about Lavinia, which might help explain why she turned out to be so mean. Lavinia puts on a good show, but the truth of the matter is that she was absolutely dreading her mother's arrival. In front of people, Lavinia and her mother seemed to have the perfect mother/daughter relationship, but behind closed doors it was a very, very different story. Tallulah Wright had always been far too self-obsessed to think about anyone other than herself.

What chance did Lavinia have with a mother like that? We might almost feel sorry for the poor girl – if she wasn't so vile to our dear friends at L'Etoile. All we can say to you is, let this be a lesson for when you have children of your own, Story-seeker. Above all, you must make them feel loved and secure, so that they grow up to be happy, caring adults, not bitter and spiteful bullies like Lucinda and Lavinia.

11

The Circus Comes to Town

'Why have they dragged us all the way over here for breakfast this morning?' Maria groaned, as she loaded her plate with two croissants and a pot of raspberry jam.

'I'm not sure, but something's going on; I've just seen Madame Ruby walking across the quad – and she's *never* up for breakfast!' Fashion Faye said, overhearing Maria.

'Oh my days, I've seen it all now,' Molly said, poking Maria and Pippa to get their attention, as suddenly the double doors swung open – seemingly by themselves. Within seconds the whole dining hall had turned to face the entrance – and the Hollywood A-Lister that was Tallulah Wright swooshed in with her nose firmly in the air.

'Do you think we should all have said *Tah-dah*?' Pippa gasped.

'If I'd known, I'd have brought my sticks and given her a drum-roll!' Lara said sarcastically.

'Honestly, anyone would think Prince Henry was back in town with all this fuss. She's just a woman who's made loads of money from talking for a living. And talking *at* people for that matter. Mum says she never really listens to anyone she's interviewing and always manages to bring the subject back to herself,' Molly said quietly.

Tallulah Wright, despite her fame and fortune, did not have the charisma that the girls imagined a real Hollywood A-Lister like Angelina Jolie might have. In fact, for all her bravado, she was shorter than the girls had expected, and if they were really horrible, slightly more dumpy!

'Mom-my!' came a cry from the back of the Ivy Room.

'Oh here we go, girls. Brace yourselves for an Oscar-winning performance,' Sally said, wincing at the thought.

'I can't look!' Molly said, throwing her hands in

front of her face – then opening her fingers for a peep.

'Mommy. I've missed you!' Lavinia had bombed across the dining room – having deliberately sat in the seat furthest from the entrance to maximise her run up. She launched herself at her mother, nearly knocking her over, in an attempt to display a happy family. But despite their best attempts to fool the audience, every L'Etoilette in the room noticed the undeniably frosty welcome TW gave her daughter.

'Tell me she didn't just air-kiss her own child!' Pippa said, rather too loudly.

'Probably didn't want to blot her lipgloss!' Autumn commented. 'What did she layer that on with this morning – a trowel?'

Suddenly Madame Ruby emerged from behind Tallulah and Lavinia and put her hand up for silence.

L'Etoilettes, thank you for gathering here this morning. I know you have a busy day ahead of you with last-minute exam preparations, but I wanted to introduce you to our very special guest, Mrs Tallulah Wright.'

The girls gave a brief round of applause.

'As has been explained to you already, Mrs Wright and her camera crew are joining us for a few very exciting days, so please would you ensure that you are as presentable and natural as I know you can be. *The TW show*'s cameras are now up and running throughout the school, so please remember our usual exceptional standards of behaviour. I know Mrs Wright is most looking forward to recording glimpses of your performance exams tomorrow, so if you do happen to be selected for that honour, do yourselves and L'Etoile proud. Good luck, L'Etoilettes and welcome, Tallulah Wright!'

'Come on, girls, let's get out of here. All this fake happiness and pretend applause is getting right on my nerves,' said Maria.

'What a way to start the day,' answered Pippa. 'I'm starting to realise how bad Sally's version of B-A-D is! I've never been so happy at the thought of locking myself away in a rehearsal room all day!'

After a restless night's sleep, exam day one came and went without too much disruption. To the first years' surprise – and for some, relief – not one of their performances was filmed by Tallulah's crew, which Molly immediately put down to Lavinia's green-eyed jealousy.

'It's not right! The only two practical pieces that

were filmed today were Luci's and Lavi's! How can Miss Hart and Madame Ruby have allowed that to happen?' Molly raved angrily, when the girls were back in their bedroom.

'We should have seen it coming, Moll,' Sally said. 'Try not to take it to heart. There'll be other chances for you to showcase your talent.'

'I know. I don't mean to sound like a little princess, Sally. It just really gets on my nerves, that's all. They shouldn't have this much power. We all deserved a chance to appear on that show,' Molly answered.

'How did you get on, anyway?' Pippa asked.

'Not bad.' 'Fine.' 'Good, I think,' came three responses all at once.

'Did you hear about poor Lara, though? Somehow, a few of the bolts on her drum-kit came loose halfway through her solo and the whole thing collapsed. The poor thing was in as many bits as her kit!' Maria said.

'Oh no, really? I can't believe I didn't hear about that. Is she OK? We could have taken her some chocolate to cheer her up, Mimi, but I can't face sneaking over to Monroe now. I'm pooped!' Molly said, wearily.

'She'll be all right. Miss Hart said she could do it again first thing tomorrow before the workshop, when she was feeling fresh – so don't worry,' Pippa said.

'Don't mention that workshop, for goodness' sake. I can't bear it. It's going to be simply awful, I just know it,' Sally said, almost tearfully.

'I know. Do you remember on the first day of term when you and the rest of 1 Beta came to our classroom and we just held our breath, waiting to see who Lucifette was going to pick on first – I reckon it's going to be like that,' Pippa said. 'You can bet your life Luci and Lavi are briefing TW as we speak.'

'Right, that's quite enough, you two!' Maria announced. 'You're going to wind each other up so badly you'll never get to sleep tonight. What will be, will be and whatever happens, we'll have each other's backs. I, for one, say we change the subject so that we can clear our heads before bed.'

Sally, Molly and Pippa looked at her blankly, unable to empty their minds enough to think of another subject.

'Hopeless! Do I have to think of everything?' Maria rolled her eyes.

Maria was tired and stressed too, Story-seeker. Not so much with the exam thing, or the workshop thing; she was just annoyed with herself that she'd not had a chance to make a start on her Gazette article and it was playing on her mind. Still, once the exams were over, she could really get cracking. The good news is her *Yours, L'Etoilette* piece about the tours – entitled '*L'ETOILE COMES UP SMELLING OF ROSES*' was getting a ton of hits and plenty of helpful feedback for her to anonymously pass on to Miss Hart.

'I know!' Molly said, relieved. 'Let's talk about the fundraiser. That's sure to lift our spirits. Where are we with the prizes, Pips?'

Pippa grabbed her school bag and pulled out a purple file with the word CALUM written across the front.

'Ah, that's so sweet, Pippa. Just imagine how he'd feel if he knew we were all thinking about him and trying to help. It's such a shame we can't let him know and invite him.'

'But that's a great idea, Molly. Why can't we do that? Let's ask Eddie to pop over to the casting studio when he's got a spare moment. You never know your luck – Calum might just be there,' Maria said, excitedly.

'Do you really think so, Mimi? I'd love that. It would be so great for him to see the evening. I think maybe we'd better speak to Mum about the best way to handle this. Perhaps she can go with Eddie and see if she can't talk him into going to a shelter – start the ball rolling with helping him to get off the streets,' Molly answered.

'Good, that's a plan then,' Maria said, already tapping away at an email to their mother.

'Where are we up to with the auction prizes, Pippa?' Sally asked. 'Have we got donation details through from everyone yet?'

'Funny you should say that; the only two I'm missing, perhaps unsurprisingly, are Luci and Lavi. As if they would waste any time thinking about anything other than themselves!' Pippa answered.

'Oh, never mind those two. I've no doubt they'll pull something amazing out of the bag just in time. They'll probably deliberately miss the printer deadline and announce their donations as last-minute prizes to gain maximum exposure and attention for themselves,' Sally added, knowing those two witches better than anyone.

'OK, so apart from you-know-who, I think we've done amazingly well. Let's see . . . ' Pippa began to run through her prize list.

'Me – the good news is that Mr Fuller has come up with a studio! He's offered it to Uncle Harry and me for three days and said he'll go along for an afternoon session to give advice on the record. Amazing!

'Fitzfoster Twins – a Fitzfoster diamond solitaire necklace. I don't even want to think what that would cost in the shop!

'Sally – a Country Pursuits Weekend with all the trimmings at the Fitzfoster pad in Sussex.

'Belle – I heard back from Miss Hart today that Madame Ruby has given the fluffy toy Twinkle idea the big thumbs-up for use both on auction night and throughout the summer mystery tours. Apparently she was so enthusiastic, she even telephoned Mr and Mrs Brown herself to make the arrangements. That's a sale that will just run and run and hopefully make a fortune for the charity way beyond the auction.

'Sofia – a chef's table for ten people at her father's Michelin-starred restaurant. And the big prize here is, it's for his flagship restaurant in Venice, Italy – AND he's paying for flights and accommodation too. How fab is that?

'Alice – Parry Parks are offering VIP membership access – and that means *free* – to any of their UK car parks for a whole year. Take it from me, that's like gold dust! Mum's always moaning about the price of parking in London!

'Lydia – oh yes, I'll tell you about her in a bit – her family have been so generous!

'Amanda – her mum, as you know, works for the prime minister and has managed to put together a money-can't-buy prize of a tour around Ten Downing Street and a quick hello with the PM himself. How cool! I don't think there's a busier man on the planet!

'Nancy – a Chelsea football shirt signed by the whole team on the day they won the European Cup Final, as Nancy's dad is the physio for the team.

'Lara and Elizabeth – a joint prize of a week's holiday at Lara's family's hotel in Barbados, and Elizabeth's mum's sorting flights with British Airways.

'Daisy – Daisy's dad is a Savile Row tailor – he quite often makes suits for the male members of the royal family. He's donating four bespoke suits – a new one for every season for the next year.

'Charlotte – Charlotte's aunt owns a chateau in the Champagne region in France and is offering business-class Eurostar travel and a four-night stay for twelve, including a private tour of the cellars.

'Corine – Corine's family owns a chain of cinemas and are offering to shut down one of their screens for a Saturday evening so that the lucky winner can take friends and family for a private viewing of a film of their choice. All the popcorn you can eat included!

'Heavenly – Heavenly's grandfather owns a London art gallery. He's offering the chance for the winner to have their portrait painted by a top British artist. He guarantees that in time the painting will be worth far more than they bid for it.

'Autumn – Autumn's father is a landscape architect and has said he will sell his services to the highest bidder and transform any outside space into a breathtaking haven for its owner.

'Faye – unbeknown to us, and I can't believe we didn't guess, Faye's mum is a big cheese at *Vogue* magazine and she's donated a fashion shoot with real *Vogue* photographers – with the possibility, if the pics are good enough, of there being a little article in the magazine!

'Betsy – Betsy's family own a musical instrument shop – specifically pianos, hence Betsy being a genius pianist, and they're donating the most gorgeous baby grand piano.

'Luci and Lavi – well, your guess is as good as mine . . . '

When Pippa finally looked up from her scribbled list, she giggled as she saw the twins and Sally, their mouths open in astonishment at the list of super-prizes she'd just read out so matter-of-factly.

'Pippa – that's just incredible. There are literally tens, if not hundreds of thousands of pounds' worth of prizes there. I can't believe it!' Molly said, as the realisation dawned of just how much money they stood to make for their charity.

'I know. I don't think I'd quite realised myself, to be honest. I've been getting notes and emails from the girls in dribs and drabs so until I read it out in one go like this, I didn't realise how amazing it sounds,' Pippa answered, grinning.

'Let's type that up over the weekend and email it to Mum so she can start work on the design of the auction programme. And why don't we send Luci and Lavi an email now to say they've got until five o'clock on Sunday to get their donations in or they won't make the programme – and they won't be part of the auction – which would be too embarrassing for words!' Maria said.

'Shall I tell them about Lydia's donation?' Sally suddenly remembered.

'Of course! Yes, I forgot that,' Pippa exclaimed.

'Lydia came up with the brilliant idea that we should have the auction out by the lake rather than inside the Kodak Hall like every L'Etoile event. I spoke to Miss Hart about it as the weather forecast for June is looking good and she thinks it's a lovely idea,' Sally began as the girls nodded in agreement.

'And even better is that Lydia's family own Ambrose Events and have said they would like to provide the backdrop and catering for the event as their donation. The theme is going to be 'A Midsummer Night's Picnic', with fairy lights draped through the trees to make it feel dreamy, and a British picnic supper – you know the sort of thing: Coronation Chicken, cold meats, pork pies, scotch eggs, champagne and loads of strawberries and cream.'

'How lovely!' Molly said, having quite forgotten all about exams. 'Maybe we can ask Faye to start running up bunting from next week. There's nothing like home-made bunting!'

'Perfect!' Sally answered. 'The only thing I might need a hand with is a witty script to announce the auction items. Mind you – your list is already a great start on that, Pippa, so thanks for that. We'll just throw in a few jokes here and there – and you'll sing at some point, Pippa, won't you?'

'Blimey!' Pippa answered in a panic. 'I'd forgotten about the entertainment side of things. Right then, once I've handed this list over on Sunday, I'll get to work.'

'Well done us!' said Maria, feeling like they'd really achieved something.

'Now not another word about the next two days. We'll get through it, no bother at all. 'Night, lovelies!'

But we know, as do you, Story-seeker, that Maria was about to be thrown into the thick of a major nightmare. Sweet dreams one and all!

12

A Twist in the Talk-Show Tail

You could have heard a pin drop as the first years sat nervously waiting for TW's talk-show workshop to begin. No one knew what to expect, but a feeling of doom hung in the air.

'Hurry up L, or we'll be missed!' Lucinda hissed to Lavinia through a crack in the twins' bedroom door.

Lavinia used her gloved hand to remove the printed history exam paper from its envelope and tuck one corner under Maria's laptop at the end of her bed.

'*Operation Cheating Fitzfoster . . .* done!' she squealed with excitement as she exited the bedroom, closing the door behind her.

The early call time for the first years to take their

seats in the hall for the workshop had given Lucinda and Lavinia the perfect opportunity to slip into Garland unseen and plant their evidence.

None of the first years thought that there was anything odd about those two arriving so much later than the rest of them. They'd already assumed they would want to make a grand entrance with TW and, for the most part, they were right!

Suddenly Tallulah Wright waltzed on stage, as half a dozen lights on cameras flashed red, to show they were recording live.

'What is that outfit?' Molly leaned forwards and whispered to Faye, who happened to be sitting in front of her.

'I know, don't. The shoulder pads are level with her eyebrows! Whatever next?' Faye whispered back, praying that her voice wouldn't be picked up on one of a hundred microphones dotted around the room.

'What you've gotta realise, ladies, is that if you want something badly enough and it's there for the taking, you just gotta go out and grab it. Don't be holding back on anyone else's account. It's your life, and you gotta live it. You're number one!' TW boomed.

'That'll be right; TW only looks out for TW!' Sally whispered to Pippa. 'I almost want to say, *poor Lavinia*.'

'Well, don't!' Maria scolded.

'So if we're ready to begin, may I have my first guest on stage please,' TW continued. 'Ladies, would you put your hands together for Mrs Audrey Butter, head of History here at L'Etoile, School for Stars.'

The girls whooped and cheered. They were fond of dotty old Butter-boots.

Audrey Butter walked in, sporting her signature yellow wellies and a new yellow-and-white polka-dot dress, looking pleased as punch.

Between us, Story-seeker, it had been a lifelong dream of Mrs Butter's for someone to consider her interesting enough to appear on their chat-show – and with the great Tallulah Wright sitting opposite her, she felt as if she'd just won the lottery!

'So, Mrs Butter, tell me where your passion for history came from,' TW asked, cocking her head to one side in a sympathetic, *I want everyone to think I'm really listening but secretly this show's all about ME*, type look.

Old Butter-boots began talking, slightly nervously

at first, taking the girls back to her days at Oxford University and a professor there by the name of Mrs Tredrea, who had inspired her. Just as she'd begun to find her confidence, TW suddenly clutched her earpiece and put up her hand for silence, with all the drama of a newsreader being fed the very latest information.

'I'm sorry to stop you there, Mrs Butter, but I'm being given, via my presenter's earpiece here . . . ' and she held it aloft for the audience to see before plugging it back in, ' . . . oh my, it's dreadful news. Ladies, this is where reality meets the world of television and I'm sorry to have to be the one to tell you . . . '

The first years gasped with anticipation, wondering what could possibly have happened.

'Sure she is!' said Sally, suspiciously. 'She's loving every second of this – look at the glee on her face!'

Suddenly the large television screen behind them came to life, showing a tweet to @twshow from @whistleblower2013.

It read:

@TWshow Urgent investigation required: L'Etoilette girl witnessed stealing exam paper in an attempt to cheat the system. Regards, @whistleblower2013

Within seconds, the hall erupted into a wall of nervous chatter and shocked faces.

'Who would dare?!' 'Silly girl!' 'Impossible!'

Everyone was too busy gossiping to notice Lavinia looking smug in the front row, tweeting her own mother from an anonymous Twitter account.

Old Butter-boots jumped up from her seat and grabbed her briefcase from Miss Hart, who was looking on in horror, wondering whether to stop the recording. But it was all happening too quickly – besides, it wasn't live television so she was quite convinced Madame Ruby would have the last word on whether the footage could be used.

The audience fell silent as old Butter-boots carefully leafed through the paperwork in a red leather box file she'd pulled from her bag.

'It's impossible, Miss Hart,' she said, a look of relief on her face. 'All the papers are here, as I thought they must be. They haven't been out of my sight for a second!'

Then she turned to TW, about to insist there had been an error, when TW clutched her earpiece for a second time.

'I'm afraid another tweet has come through. We're not able to disclose its contents on the screen; however I do have a roaming reporter on the ground,

Ben Bainley, and I can cut to him now for further investigation.'

Tallulah Wright paused, relishing the fact that her audience were eating out of her hands. It was too good! Not being able to resist, and against her producer's instructions, she revealed a bit more. 'There is one more thing I can tell you, ladies. The suspect is a first-year girl and I do believe that she is sitting in this very room.'

The room exploded into a din: 'No!' 'Impossible!'

'Ben Bainley, are you receiving?' TW called out, even more loudly.

The face of a reporter flashed up onto the TV screen. 'Yes, Tallulah, I can hear you loud and clear. I'm here in the Garland corridor, following a description given us by @whistleblower2013.'

'Supercalifragilisticexpialidocious!' Pippa exclaimed in a whisper.

'This is looking B-A-D!' Maria agreed, with an overwhelming feeling that something dreadful was about to happen.

The cameras followed as Ben Bainley disappeared down a dark corridor – driving the girls crazy as they couldn't tell immediately whose room he was passing. Suddenly he stopped outside a door and knocked. No answer. Then as Miss Coates came into view, with the Garland master bedroom key, Maria suddenly spotted a familiar dent in the door frame which she and Eddie had made accidentally when they dragged that heavy chocolate trunk into their room at the start of term.

'Oh, Moll. It's our room!' she said in a whisper.

Before Molly had time to say a word, the door was thrown open and Ben, Miss Coates and a couple of other TV crew members had started rummaging around for evidence.

By this time the whole room was looking right at Maria, Molly, Pippa and Sally – but the girls were speechless. They simply couldn't believe what was unfolding in front of their eyes.

TW couldn't resist creating a little more drama around the events.

'While Ben investigates further, I can tell you, people, that the girl in question was seen removing the papers from Mrs Butter's red folder by another student, who wishes to remain anonymous . . .'

'Tallulah, can you hear me?' Ben suddenly asked gingerly, and everyone's gaze was transfixed once again on the large TV screen.

'Yes, back with you, Ben. Tell us, what have you found?' TW said hurriedly.

'I think this is what we're looking for,' Ben answered, bending down and lightly tugging at the document sticking out from under Maria's laptop (using gloves, of course, so as not to disturb any fingerprints).

'But that's impossible!' Maria blurted out from the audience. 'I've never seen that piece of paper before in my life!' Suddenly the cameras had swung round to the twins, catching their reaction.

Totally ignoring Maria's outcry, TW marched on with her investigation. 'Would you kindly bring the evidence to the studio . . . er, Kodak Hall please, Ben.'

Out of the blue Miss Hart stood up and the cameras immediately focused on her.

'With all due respect, Mrs Wright, I would request that filming be suspended for the next hour or so pending further investigation. I find it very hard to believe that something so dreadful is true of any of our students, and would like to get to the bottom of this myself before any unnecessary damage is done to the girls' reputations.'

TW turned red with anger. 'Helen – you don't mind if I call you Helen, do you?'

'Actually it's Miss Hart, Mrs Wright, and I am afraid I must insist most forcefully. SHUT DOWN those cameras IMMEDIATELY!' she boomed in a way the girls had never heard before.

The audience watched in shock as, one by one, the red recording lights went out.

'Go, Miss Hart!' someone whispered from the front row as Maria thought she might actually faint.

'First years, you are dismissed for early lunch, and not a word of this is to be discussed outside this hall. Is that understood?' Miss Hart continued.

The girls nodded in silence and immediately began to file out of the room.

'Maria, Molly, Pippa and Sally, would you be kind enough to accompany me to my office?' Miss Hart said, but this time with the gentleness they were used to from their favourite teacher.

Moments later, the four forever friends had been through the interrogation of their lives and for once, they truly knew absolutely nothing about the mischief that had occurred. Maria even went so far as to say how devastated she was that after everything they'd got up to since arriving at L'Etoile, she was about to be expelled for something that she'd had no part in. Molly and Sally were both in tears and Pippa was trying to be strong for all four of them, pleading with Miss Hart to believe Maria. It truly was the worst day of their lives.

Miss Hart asked the girls to wait quietly in her office while she made a couple more enquiries.

The fact is, Story-seeker, that Miss Hart no more thought the girls were guilty of cheating than she thought Tallulah Wright had a heart of gold. This belief was reinforced by speaking to the girls and seeing them almost collapse with despair when she questioned them about what had happened.

'Audrey, I simply don't believe Maria would do this – do you?' Miss Hart asked the bewildered history teacher in the staffroom. 'Apart from the fact that she has no need to cheat in the exams, the way the whole thing unfolded and the timing of it is too convenient for my liking. It made far too interesting television for it not to be suspicious.'

'Do you know, Helen, I've been thinking the very same thing myself,' Old Butter-boots said, patting her unruly hair.

'But the fact remains that someone, if not Maria, then someone else, managed to get their hands on that exam file long enough to take a photo of your history paper and make a copy. Are you absolutely sure you didn't leave the red box unattended at any time?'

'Quite sure, Helen! It's been in my briefcase, which has been at my side for the past week so that as soon as members of staff handed me their subject papers, I could file them away safely immediately. One thing I know for sure is that it didn't happen before Monday evening,' old Butter-boots continued.

'Oh, how can you be sure, Audrey?' Miss Hart asked.

'Because I stayed late in the staffroom to compose my history papers on Monday afternoon. I had a dinner date and thought I'd use the time after school to finish off and then go straight from here.'

'I see,' Miss Hart said thoughtfully. 'And what time would that have been?'

'I left at seven o'clock on the dot – actually it was more like quarter past seven by the time I got to my car as I forgot something in the staffroom and had to nip back for . . . oh, my goodness me!' she cried. 'Oh dear, dear, dear. It must have been then. That's the only time . . . oh golly.'

And poor Old Butter-boots poured her heart out about catching a glimpse of her crazy hair in the corridor mirror, leaving her bags and the exam file in the hall for a split second while she rushed back to the staffroom to grab her hairbrush and hairspray.

'Oh, Audrey. It must have been then!' Miss Hart sighed. 'Someone must have been hiding in the corridor, waiting for an opportunity. I'll bet they couldn't believe their luck!'

'I'm so sorry, Helen.'

'You're not to worry,' Miss Hart said, putting an arm around her yellow polka-dot shoulder. I've got a plan to put this right. Don't repeat a word of what you've just told me to anyone, all right? I'll see you back in the studio in half an hour. Would you gather the girls and make sure they're back in their seats for then too?'

'Absolutely, Helen. I just can't believe I was so careless.'

Knock, knock.

'Dad, it's me, Helen. Are you there?'

As Miss Hart pushed open the caretaker's office door, she was met by a very enthusiastic Twinkle. Mr Hart hadn't had a chance to take her for her morning run around so she was desperate for some fun.

'Hello, Twinkle, is your and my father here?' Miss Hart said, smiling for the first time that day.

'Over here,' came a muffled voice from the corner.

'Been trying to get this blinking plug working; can't imagine what's wrong with it. I've tried changing the fuse, rewiring it, but—'

'Dad! I'm sorry but I'm in a hurry and a bit of a pickle for that matter! One of my girls is in trouble and I'm hoping you can help.'

'Of course, Helen. Who's in trouble?' David Hart said immediately, putting down his tools.

'It's Maria Fitzfoster,' Miss Hart said, unable to hide the desperation in her voice, and in under a minute, she'd explained the whole horrendous situation.

'Why that little tweeter . . . You wait until I get my hands on her! You don't go around framing innocent girls!' Mr Hart said protectively. He'd be forever thankful to those Fitzfoster girls for bringing him Twinkle.

'Dad, did you install those security cameras at the weekend like I asked? Please say you did,' Miss Hart pleaded.

'Of course I did, Helen. I have to admit I thought you were mad at the time, given the number of TV cameras we've got around the school this week, but now it seems you were right to be careful – especially with all the extra people we'll have wandering around the school grounds with the upcoming Lost Rose tours.'

'Exactly! And I'm so glad I did now this has happened. Can you check the tape for the staffroom corridor on Monday evening between seven o'clock and half past? I think that's when our criminal managed to get their hands on the exam papers. If there's any justice, we'll have caught them in the act on film!'

'Give me five minutes, darling. You really are a very clever girl, Helen Hart. You must get it from your dear old dad!' He went over to the audiovisual cabinet to scroll back through the security footage.

13

You've Been Framed!

Now if you think for a moment, Story-seeker, that those first-year girls could keep from talking about the TV exam episode, you're mistaken. Could you resist gossip that good? We're happy to say that they did manage to keep it to a whisper though, so discussions didn't go any further than the first years.

'I just don't believe Maria would do it,' Betsy said to Charlotte and Sofia at lunch.

'I know! Anyone but Maria. She's a genius. Why would she need to cheat? It just doesn't make any sense,' Charlotte whispered back.

'Exactly!' Nancy said, putting her tray down next to

Betsy's. 'If it had been anyone else – you girls included – I couldn't have been so sure – but Maria? No way!'

'Thanks for the vote of confidence, Nancy,' Betsy said, hurt that one of her own friends thought she might cheat.

'You know what I mean, Betsy. You hate maths and are always saying how much you struggle with it. If it had been a maths paper that had gone missing, I couldn't have helped but wonder if it was you. But Maria Fitzfoster – she hasn't got a *struggling* bone in her body!' Nancy explained. 'Put it another way – if she had decided to cheat, she'd never have got caught in a million years, or been as stupid as to leave a copy under her laptop! She'd have memorised it with that brilliant photographic memory of hers and then made any trace of evidence disappear somewhere in cyberspace!'

'Well, that only leaves one explanation then, doesn't it?' Charlotte whispered back. 'Someone has set her up!'

Lucinda and Lavinia listened intently to the conspiracy theories circulating around them. They even joined in a couple of conversations so it looked like they were as confused as everyone else. Lavinia felt invincible, but Lucinda was a bit worried that no one would believe the hype about Maria. She could have kicked herself for not suggesting they frame Molly instead. It would have been far less obvious and would have hurt Maria more, if anything.

As the girls were ushered back into the Kodak Hall by old Butter-boots, they were surprised to see Miss Hart sitting in the guest chair in front of TW, with a make-up artist busy powdering the shine off her nose.

Maria, Molly, Pippa and Sally were sitting together in the front row wondering what Miss Hart was up to.

Maria looked white with fear. 'What's going on, do you think?' she asked her sister.

Molly gripped her twin's hand. 'I don't know, Mimi, but I've never seen Miss Hart look more in control and she's clearly told the cameras to resume recording, so let's just cross our fingers and hope that she's going to sort this whole mess out.'

Maria didn't look convinced.

'I just know that Lucifette and Lavatory are behind it all!' Pippa whispered. 'No one else would dare to set you up like this.'

'I'm with you there, Pips,' Sally agreed. 'And it wouldn't surprise me if TW is in on it herself – just to make exciting television!'

Just as Maria was about to answer, Miss Hart

called out to her.

'Maria, would you join me on the stage for a moment?' she asked softly. Something in Miss Hart's eyes as she said it made Maria feel safe.

Tallulah Wright couldn't believe her luck when Miss Hart suggested Maria join the interview panel. What teacher would throw one of their own students to the wolves, even if they were a thieving little cheat?

'So, Miss Fitzfoster . . . Maria . . . you don't mind if I call you Maria?' TW began, but she didn't wait for an answer. 'Without wishing this to be a public trial, can you explain to me and everyone at home how that history paper came to be in your possession?'

Maria was suddenly purple with embarrassment. She must have read Miss Hart all wrong. How could she have done this to her? The room was silent. All she could hear were muffled sniffs coming from Molly's direction.

As she opened her mouth to protest her innocence, Miss Hart put her hand on her shoulder to silence her. 'If I may interrupt at this point, Tallulah . . . you don't mind if I call you Tallulah, do you?' she mocked, just as TW had belittled her and poor Maria.

'Upon discovery of the history paper in one of my student's bedrooms, the L'Etoile staff and I have done a little searching ourselves to find a more accurate explanation for what has happened here today. You see, Tallulah . . . ' and she paused for effect, 'Maria Fitzfoster is, without question, the most intelligent girl L'Etoile has ever had the pleasure of teaching.'

Maria couldn't hold back the tears, at which point Molly flew to her sister's side.

'So you will appreciate the confusion and disbelief that has engulfed the entire year group and teaching staff, given your anonymous tweeter's bizarre accusation,' Miss Hart continued.

'Helen, dear,' TW condescended. 'You cannot deny the evidence – the witness, the tweeted message and the physical paperwork found under Miss Fitzfoster's laptop.'

'I'm sorry to tell you, Tallulah *dear*, that your so-called witness may indeed turn out to be the actual culprit. If I may draw your attention to Exhibit A – a recording from a security camera, showing the corridor outside the staffroom on the evening we believe the document to have been copied.'

Everyone turned to watch the TV screen where Ben Bainley had appeared an hour earlier with his version of events. There was old Butter-boots emerging from the staffroom with her bags, and the red exam file tucked under her arm. The audience was transfixed. They watched Mrs Butter stop to check her appearance in the huge mirror, glance around, put her possessions down on the hall-stand and nip back to the staffroom.

Suddenly a gasp went up as the unmistakable skunk-like hair-do of Lucinda Marc— no, hang on a minute, it wasn't Lucinda at all but her evil twin Lavinia Wright – was seen darting out from behind a curtain over to the red box, lifting the lid and taking a photo of both sides of the top document on her phone. Then she whizzed back to her hiding place just as old Butter-boots re-emerged from the staffroom, none the wiser!

The room was silent, but no one was more aghast than the scheming thief's mother, our delightful chat-show host Tallulah Wright.

Well, at least her reaction shows she had no idea about all this, Miss Hart thought to herself, before speaking.

'Tallulah, I appreciate this might be difficult for you to see, but I'm afraid I had very little choice, given the very public nature of this matter so far. The way you announced the whole situation with the cameras rolling, it seemed only natural to bring the *true* culprit to justice in a similarly public manner,' Miss Hart said.

Tallulah's face was like thunder, her eyes darting from Miss Hart to her red-faced daughter. For the first time in her life, she was at a complete loss for words.

'Lavinia, may I see your phone, please?' asked Miss Hart.

Lavinia got up from her seat. Even she realised it was pointless to even attempt denying anything when her every move had been caught on camera. She couldn't believe it!

'Thank you, Lavinia,' Miss Hart said, 'for having the sense not to make this any worse for yourself.'

As soon as she turned on the phone, the anonymous twitter account flashed up on the screen with her messages to her own mother.

'I think you'll find everything you need regarding our mystery tweeter on your daughter's phone, Tallulah,' Miss Hart said, holding out Lavinia's phone. But TW was too furious to acknowledge anyone or anything.

'May I also suggest that we put a stop to filming now, Mrs Wright? I can't imagine you'll be too keen for this episode of *The TW Show* to be aired on your return to

LA. One thing I am certain of, however, is that you and your daughter will be keen to leave L'Etoile as soon as possible. Are there any arrangements I can make for you?'

The first years watched in absolute disbelief and secret delight as the celebrity mother viciously grabbed her daughter and disappeared from the stage. Lucinda sat very much alone, and in complete silence.

Once again, Miss Hart addressed the group. 'L'Etoilettes, I would like us to move on from what has happened here today. Sincere apologies must be extended to Maria in particular, but also Molly, Pippa and Sally who have been through a traumatic couple of hours under the eye of suspicion. I would like to reiterate that they had nothing whatsoever to do with Miss Wright's plot to frame them for cheating.' She turned to Maria and the girls. 'I'm very sorry for everything you've been through today, ladies.'

'As you know,' she continued, 'your contributions in today's workshop were due to give you a grade to form part of your final mark for the term. In view of the disastrous events of this morning, I've no choice but to award every single one of you an A-grade and dismiss you now to give you plenty of study time this afternoon ahead of tomorrow's academic exams.'

'Yessss'es to A-grades and 'nooooooo's to more studying rumbled around the room as the girls got up to leave. They couldn't wait to get outside and discuss every second of what had just happened.

As the girls filed out, Miss Hart pulled Lucinda aside. 'Lucinda, if you wouldn't mind staying behind, I have some things to discuss with you.'

What the rest of the year and staff hadn't been shown on the tape was that Lavinia had not been alone, hiding in that staffroom corridor. Lucinda was quite clearly seen arriving, hiding and departing with her. However, given that she hadn't actually been caught in the act herself, Miss Hart felt it would have been unfair to expel her alongside Lavinia. She thought this information would be much better used to issue Lucinda with a stark warning about her behaviour towards her studies, her fellow students and the teaching staff.

'You see, Lucinda, although I have all the evidence I need to prove that you were at Miss Wright's side during this whole hideous affair, I feel that perhaps you were unfairly led astray on this occasion and I am willing to give you a second chance.'

Lucinda was mortified to be on the back foot, but relieved not to be in the sort of trouble she knew she deserved to be in.

'Yes, Miss,' she answered meekly.

'I want you on your best behaviour for the remainder of the term, Miss Marciano. If the slightest hint of any bullying reaches me in connection with you, that security tape will find itself on Madame Ruby's desk quicker than you can say "not guilty"! Is that understood, Lucinda?'

Lucinda nodded. It wasn't staying at L'Etoile that she cared about. But she so wanted that part in the Warner Brothers film. Who knew what damage expulsion from the great School for Stars could do?

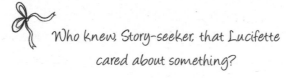

Who knew, Story-seeker, that Lucifette cared about something?

'I couldn't believe it when that film crew stopped outside our bedroom door! And then when they found that document under my laptop, I was so horrified, I couldn't think straight,' Maria said, slightly more colour in her cheeks now that she'd been cleared of cheating. 'Of course it had to be that horror-hog, Lavi.'

'Told you she makes Lucifette look like an angel!' Sally said.

'Yeah, well, I don't think she's that innocent in this whole thing, either. I reckon she was in it with Lavatory up to her highlights!' said Pippa.

'You're so right, Mimi!' exclaimed Molly. 'There's no way she wasn't crouching behind that curtain as well. But as usual, she's been too clever to do her own dirty work!'

'Well, whoever was involved I'm just glad they couldn't pin it on any of us!' Maria answered, still dizzy with relief. 'How do we always manage to get ourselves in such scrapes? And this one was none of our doing. It just sort of happened around us!'

'Thank goodness for Miss Hart and her common sense, that's what I say. What do you say we ask Mum if we can get her a gold star necklace with an H in the middle to say thanks for all her help this year?' asked Molly.

'Brilliant idea!' Maria answered, forever grateful to the teacher who had saved her – again – that morning.

'I can't believe we've got a whole day of serious work tomorrow,' Pippa groaned. 'Don't suppose you've got any other exam papers tucked under your mattress do you, Maria?'

'You wish!' Maria answered, launching a well-aimed slipper in Pippa's direction.

14

There's No Place Like Home

Now you might think this is weird, Story-seeker,
especially for our girls, but there was nothing very
interesting or eventful about examination day three.
And to be perfectly honest – what a relief! The events
of the talk-show workshop had been quite enough
excitement for that week. So if it's all right with you,
we'll just tell you that the girls got through it in their
own stressed or chilled-out way and moved on to
happier things! The fundraiser!

'This is sooooo exciting!' Molly squealed in delight
as she opened the curtains the week of the first
years' charity auction. 'I can't believe how many

delivery trucks there are! Lydia's family has pulled out all the stops for us, haven't they?'

'I know. Just think, if we had had to pay for an event like this, it would have cost a fortune. There wouldn't have been any money left from the auction to send to the charity. It's so kind of them,' Pippa agreed, leaping over to the window to see the last AMBROSE EVENTS lorry disappear down the track to the lake.

'Have you seen Maria, Pips?' Molly asked, looking over at her sister's empty bed. 'Her bed's been empty every morning for the past two weeks since the exams finished. I'm worried about her. She's working too hard.'

'You know her better than anyone, Moll – but I reckon she's camping in the library again, working on her *Gazette* article before classes start. I can't remember when the deadline is but it must be any day now. I'm pretty sure it's due in around the time of the auction,' Pippa answered.

'She should have let us chip in and help her. If we've learned anything this year, it's that four heads are better than one!' Molly said. 'I'm going to nip over to the library and see her now, before class.'

'But you've only plaited one bunchie,' Pippa

answered in astonishment. 'Molly – you never go out in public like that!'

'I don't care what I look like today. My sister needs me, Pippa!' And with that she ran off down the corridor, golden curls flapping wildly on one side of her head, plait bouncing on the other.

'Did I actually just hear those words come from the immaculate Miss Molly's mouth?' Pippa said to Sally, who was equally flabbergasted. In the whole year they'd known Molly Fitzfoster, they'd never seen her leave their bedroom less than perfect!

'Molly, you are cute, but I'm fine – honestly,' Maria said, clutching her sister's hand. 'Don't you get it? This is the opportunity I've been waiting for. If I had help from you guys it wouldn't feel as though I was entering this competition fair and square.'

Molly didn't look convinced.

'Want to have a read? Maybe then you'll feel better,' Maria continued, swivelling the laptop around for Molly to see.

Molly couldn't believe her luck. She'd been dying to see what Maria had been writing and couldn't wait to experience their first-year adventures all over again in

Maria's words. By the time she got to the end, she had the biggest grin on her face.

'Maria, I know we say it all the time, but you're sooo clever. This is a piece of genius. Mummy and Daddy will be so proud of you when they read it. I especially love the way you've interviewed *Yours, L'Etoilette!* No one would ever guess she's you!' Molly said, giving her sister the biggest hug. 'If you don't win this competition, I'd certainly like to read the article that does. There's no way it can be as exciting or emotional as this is.'

Maria thought she might cry. Nothing had ever meant more to her in her life . . . not even solving the mystery of the Lost Rose.

'Oh, Molly, do you really think so? I just want it to be the best it can possibly be.'

'Well, I'd say you're nearly there. By the time you've added your final diary entry about the auction, it'll be perfect. Now come on, or we'll be late.'

And with that, the girls ran off to class, trailing their satchels happily behind them.

'Come on, girls!' Sally called from where she was sitting, practically cheek to cheek with the wall on one side and the twins on the other. It wasn't one of the bigger Mozart rooms!

'Sorrreee!' Pippa replied. 'We're nearly there, honest. I know you've got loads to do, girls, but I desperately need your opinion on this new song before we do it at the auction. It's called "There's No Place like Home". Gosh, I'm so nervous. It's a bit different! I really hope you like it!'

As soon as the exams were over, Pippa had spent every waking minute, in and out of class, working on a new song. She wanted the lyrics to reflect the loneliness of living on the streets and for the sound to be something new and fresh. Finally, inspired by the beautiful operatic harmonies of Charlotte and Sofia floating across the quad one evening, and her own pop style, Pippa had written a song that mixed the heady world of opera with the edgy world of pop music. She couldn't ever remember being so terrified about a reaction – except perhaps when she'd been standing at the back of the Kodak Hall that night of the Christmas Gala, waiting to sing her very first song, 'Life's a Dream'.

Suddenly there was a knock at the door.

'Come in!' Charlotte called.

'Thought you might need a hand,' Lara grinned, waving her drumsticks in the air.

Then Betsy appeared behind her, followed by Lydia dragging her double bass and Daisy with her bassoon.

Pippa's face was a picture. 'Girls! What are you doing here? We decided it would be easier on everyone if we just performed this song to track rather than dragging you down to rehearsals. It's been so busy with the exams – we're all exhausted!'

'Are you kidding? And miss the chance for another Pippa Burrows triumph on a L'Etoile stage? Not likely!' Lydia giggled.

'But I haven't written up any sheet music for you,' Pippa answered in a panic, looking at her watch. 'And there's just no time before the auction.'

'Chill, Pippa,' Charlotte cried, leaping over to her bag and pulling out a wodge of annotated music paper. 'Sofia and I have been plotting this with our girl band since you first played us this magnificent track and we've written our own parts. We all agreed it would sound so much better live. So SUR-PRISE!'

'Oh, my goodness, I don't know what to say!' Pippa exclaimed, touched by their support.

Everyone in the room grinned at each other before shouting, 'SUPERCALIFRAGILISTICEXPIALIDOCIOUS!'

Pippa couldn't help but laugh this time. What friends!

As the band settled into their positions and began to play, the thumping pop tune and Pippa's soulful vocals, combined with the floating operatic harmonies of Charlotte and Sofia, was like nothing the girls had ever heard before.

'Pip-pa!' Molly exclaimed when they'd finished. 'I didn't think you'd ever compose anything to top "Life's a Dream", but I do believe you have!'

'I even forgot about my article for a whole three minutes!' Maria joined in. 'And that's quite a feat right now – believe me, Pippa. That song truly was genius!'

'It's just so different,' Sally agreed. 'Like chalk meets cheese and makes clotted cream.'

The girls laughed. Such a daft thing to say but they knew exactly what she meant.

'Hurray!' Charlotte and Sofia cried in unison.

Pippa was speechless. She felt so proud of herself and her girls. Life just kept on surprising her. Long may it continue!

15

Stage Fright Blues

'How do you spell "oss-pishus"?' Sally said, throwing the question out to the room as she sat frantically amending her script on Maria's laptop. It was the evening before the big fundraiser and her nerves were getting the better of her.

'A-u-s-p-i-c-i-o-u-s,' Maria spelled. 'I think ...' she paused, grabbing her dictionary to double-check. 'But, Sally, what are you changing now? I loved the draft you sent me earlier. It was perfect as it was. If you try to be too clever, you'll only end up getting tongue-tied on the night – especially using words none of us can even spell, let alone say.'

Sally looked thoughtful as she read through her

script for the four-billionth time.

'Yes, maybe you're right. But I just don't want to sound like a dork! I've never been centre-stage like this before and the nerves are killing me. What if I don't even make it to the stage? I can't eat, I can't sleep, I can't spell . . . !'

'Sally,' Molly said calmly, taking her hand. 'Look over there at that beautiful dress.'

Sally looked over at the wardrobe where Molly's latest *www.looklikeastar.com* purchase was hanging. It was all hers. A beautiful gift from her beautiful friends.

'You love it, right?'

Sally nodded.

'You said you felt like a superstar in it, right?'

Sally nodded again, a faint smile on her lips.

'Now look at yourself in the mirror.'

Sally looked at the unfamiliar, pretty face staring back at her. Molly had spent all afternoon testing out new looks on Sally, Maria and Pippa for the big day to follow. 'You're not telling me you don't feel like a million dollars right now, Sal?'

Sally grinned.

'Right then. I don't want to hear another word of self-doubt from you, Miss HWTM.'

Sally looked confused.

'*Hostess with the Mostess,*' Maria rescued her.

Molly continued, oblivious. 'You look amazing, Sal, and that's what you were most worried about. Your writing is brilliant; we've all been through that script with a fine-tooth comb and it's perfect – funny when it should be, poignant – and don't ask me how to spell that! – when it should be. You will be wonderful, I promise you.'

'And besides,' Maria agreed. 'Moll and I know the script inside out too, so should the worst happen, we'll be right there at your side, to help you through it. And you know how good Molly is at making things appear as if they were supposed to happen a certain way all along! Honestly. We're in this together, Sally.'

Sally had never felt so loved and part of something.

'Shall we give it to her now, Mimi?' Molly asked Maria.

'I'd say now is perfect!' Maria answered as Molly unlocked the chocolate trunk and handed Sally a familiar-looking little red box.

Sally gasped in surprise. 'A present, for me? But you've already given me so much.'

'Yes, but this is from all of us, Sal. Open it,' Molly said as she grabbed Pippa's and Maria's hands.

Sally tugged at the bow and lifted the lid, and there, twinkling back at her, was her very own gold star necklace with her 'S' initial in the centre.

'Like we said, Sally. You're part of the gang now – and we're in this together!' Maria said.

'Oooh, I love you guys. I honestly don't know how I survived so long without you!' Sally said, eyes glistening with tears. 'This star means the absolute world to me. Thank you so much.'

'You're so welcome Sally. Now step away from that script and let's get this show on the road!!'

'Can we get some sleep first?' Pippa asked, her voice hoarse from rehearsing in the open air down by the lake.

'I hope so,' Molly yawned, climbing into bed. 'I can't wait to see Mum and Dad tomorrow, too. It seems like an age since Easter. So much has happened . . . ' She paused for a moment. 'It's just a shame that Mum never managed to track Calum down.'

'I know, Moll. If only he knew how hard we've worked to try and help him and others like him.'

'Can't be helped, Mimi. We've had so much going on this term, it's a wonder we've managed to pull this event together so brilliantly. Now CO and turn that light off. It's late.'

Molly felt sad and frustrated. It would have been the icing on the cake to have had Calum there. After exhausting every possible way of tracking him down, Molly and their mum had finally given up. Some things just weren't meant to be.

'Please let me sleep, please let me sleep, please let me sleep . . . ' she said to herself, over and over until finally she nodded off.

16

Auction Sur-prizes!

'Mr and Mrs Fitzfoster!' Madame Ruby exclaimed as she made a beeline for the Fitzfoster Bentley, which had just pulled up. She practically drop-kicked the ever-obliging Eddie out of the way so that she could hold Linda Fitzfoster's door open for her.

'Madame Ruby,' Linda Fitzfoster said. 'Delightful to see you again. You're looking well.'

Madame Ruby flushed the same colour as her signature scarlet lipstick.

'Good evening, Madame Ruby,' Brian Fitzfoster said as he strolled over to his wife. 'I trust our girls have had a somewhat *less adventurous* term, this term?'

You know and we know, Story-seeker, that Mr Fitzfoster couldn't be prouder of his mischievous twin girls. He admired their spirit and all the while they managed to talk themselves out of the scrapes they got themselves into, they need not worry about being scolded by their doting dad!

'But of course, Mr Fitzfoster. I can assure you, this term has been much less eventful than the last, but not without achievement,' Madame Ruby went on, discussing things like the *Gazette* competition as she personally escorted her star couple to the lakeside.

'Would you just look at this place!' Molly said as she pirouetted around the tables. 'I couldn't imagine a more magical setting for this *Midsummer Night's Dream* themed evening. Lydia's family are incredible at their job. It really feels as if I'm in the woods with the forest fairies.'

'For once, Moll, you're not exaggerating!' Maria said. 'Goodness knows how many hundreds of fairy lights have been strung through the trees to get this effect. We absolutely must get Lydia to introduce her parents to Mum and Dad.'

All around, first years and staff members were scurrying like rabbits, each with an important job to do. Everyone had a role, from stage management to table management; from prize props to collecting prizewinners' cheques. Thankfully, Ambrose Events had provided an army of catering and waiting staff, so no student was at risk of dropping a bowl of strawberries and cream in anyone's lap!

'Molly, can you pass me one of those auction programmes out of that grey box, please,' Sally said, twitching.

'But you've got your own script, Sal, with the list on. I'd just work from that if I were—'

'Pleeeease, Moll,' Sally begged. 'Just got this awful feeling I've missed something.'

Both Molly and Sally read down the auction prize list. It was like a list of dreams.

✳ L'ETOILE ✳
SCHOOL FOR STARS
FIRST-YEAR CHARITY AUCTION OF PRIZES

✳ ✳ ✳

LOT 1 *Three days in a top recording studio with award-winning songwriter Pippa Burrows, producer Harry Burrows, overseen by Emmett Fuller, Head of Universal Music.*

LOT 2   A selection of exclusive Hollywood movie memorabilia
from the Marciano Vaults, including a Michael Jackson white
glove.

LOT 3   A Country Pursuits weekend at the fully-staffed Wilton
House in West Sussex for twelve guests (inclusive of all meals and
refreshments).

LOT 4   A chef's table for ten people at the great Italian chef
Antonio Russo's Michelin-starred restaurant in Venice, Italy
(inclusive of all flights and accommodation for a two-night
weekend stay).

LOT 5   VIP membership access to any Parry Parks Car Park in the
UK for a whole year.

LOT 6   A private tour of 10 Downing Street for a family, including
a personal welcome from the prime minister.

LOT 7   A Chelsea football shirt signed by the whole team from their
win on Cup Final Day.

LOT 8   A week's holiday for six at the Sandy Palace Resort,
Barbados, including business-class return flights with British
Airways.

LOT 9   Four exquisite men's suits – a new one for every season –
courtesy of royal tailor Mansfield Tailoring, Savile Row.

LOT 10   A four-night stay for twelve people at the beautiful
French Château Chandon in the Champagne region (inclusive of
business-class Eurostar travel, a champagne banquet and a private
tour of the cellars).

LOT 11   All the films you can watch and popcorn you can eat at
The Old Cinema, London's West End. Take up to 200 friends and
family for a private cinematic experience on a Saturday of your
choice. The cinema will be closed to the public in your honour!

LOT 12   Sit for a portrait by a young up-and-coming British artist.
The world-famous Red Gallery in London guarantees that, in
time, this portrait will be worth far more than you've paid for it!

LOT 13   The landscape architect Donald Costello will transform
any outside space into a haven for you and your family. No expense
will be spared to achieve the garden of your dreams.

LOT 14   Become Vogue's next top model with your own fashion
shoot, with a picture to appear in the magazine itself.

LOT 15   A baby grand piano.

LOT 16   A signature Fitzfoster eight-carat diamond solitaire
necklace in a platinum setting.

*   *   *

SINCERE THANKS TO ALL PRIZE DONORS, TO AMBROSE
EVENTS LTD FOR CREATING THIS EVENT AND TO BELLE'S
TOYBOX LTD FOR THE FLUFFY TWINKLE PUPPIES.
WE COULDN'T HAVE DONE IT WITHOUT YOU!

'See, I knew it! There's an extra prize that's been added in – the Marciano one. I didn't even know about that!' Sally shouted, blotting the sweat from her brow. 'How have I missed that one?'

'Oh, Sally, I'm sorry,' Pippa said, having overheard the commotion. 'It totally slipped my mind. Lucifette emailed me yesterday afternoon – just before our dress rehearsal – with that prize. We all knew she'd come up with something last-minute. I just forwarded the email straight over to Mrs Fitzfoster so she could tell the printers.' Pippa felt terrible. She knew only too well what it was like to be thrown off course before a performance.

Seeing how worried Pippa looked, Sally pulled herself together. 'It's fine, Pips. You've got enough on your plate. I know about it now and that's all that matters.'

'Bravo!' Molly shouted. 'That's the spirit, Sal! Quick girls, let's take our positions; the guests are starting to take their seats.'

17

Going Once . . . Going Twice . . . Sold!

'Mum. Uncle Harry!' Pippa squealed as she spied her mum and uncle gathered around the seating plan.

'Pippa!' Mrs Burrows hugged her daughter tightly. 'Harry, would you look at her? Isn't she a picture in this aquamarine dress?'

Pippa glowed with pride and happiness. This was the first opportunity her mum and Uncle Harry had had to come and watch a L'Etoile event.

As Uncle Harry cuddled his niece, Sally came bounding up with someone who could only have been her mother. Apart from a couple of wrinkles around the eyes, Sally and Maggie Sudbury were one and the same person!

'Sally!' Pippa gushed. 'Is this your mum? I can't believe how alike you are!' She paused, taking in the faces of mother and daughter. 'Sally, Mrs Sudbury, this is my mum, Olivia, and my uncle, Harry.'

'So good to meet you, Olivia,' Sally's mother said warmly. 'And please, call me Maggie.' Maggie Sudbury felt immediately comfortable with the Burrows. She'd been terrified of meeting only a load of pushy, wealthy mothers, but there was a friendliness about Olivia and Harry Burrows which put her at ease.

'Mum, Dad! Everyone's here! Come and meet them. You're all on the same table,' Maria cried as she spied the Burrows and the Sudburys deep in conversation.

Madame Ruby knew when it was time to leave her VIP parents to their own devices and reluctantly mumbled some excuse as she swept off to greet the next guests.

'Blimey, Dad! I'm really sorry about that. She's not as bad as you think, honestly, but she just can't help herself around you,' Maria apologised.

'Mimi, did you just stick up for old Ruby?' Molly said in surprise.

'I suppose I did,' Maria blushed. 'She's been pretty decent to me this term to be honest – and last term actually. Anyway, never mind that. I'm dying to meet Uncle Harry!'

As the Fitzfosters embraced the Burrows – *don't forget, Story-seeker, they already knew Maggie, their newest employee, who'd come down with them in the car from the country* – Molly thought to herself how happy she felt. Finally, the four best friends' families were together and the circle of friendship was complete. It wasn't long before everyone was tucking into their *very British picnic* supper, chatting through puffs of icing sugar being shaken onto strawberries dripping with cream, and loving every second of their *Midsummer Night's Dream* experience.

'Ladies and gentlemen,' Madame Ruby paused towards the end of her welcoming speech. 'There is little left for me to say before I hand you over to Miss Sally Sudbury, who will be your hostess for the evening, but to hope that you enjoy the rest of the evening and give as generously as you possibly can.

'One thing I would like to mention is that you can see at each place setting you have been given a fluffy "Twinkle" puppy courtesy of Belle's Toybox Ltd. Twinkle is L'Etoile's faithful guard dog and her main role is as gatekeeper to our Lost Rose. If you would like to take your fluffy Twinkle home with you, please pop a donation in the box on your table. Another brilliant fundraising idea from your first-year girls, which we plan to incorporate into our summer Legend of the Lost Rose mystery tours, thus extending the fundraising way beyond the proceeds raised this evening! Should any of you have any questions regarding the summer tours, incidentally, I am proud to say that the three super-sleuth L'Etoilettes who uncovered the Lost Rose are indeed among the first-year students here this evening, so please do not hesitate to approach one of them or me for a chat. I'm sure you'll agree that exciting times lie ahead, beginning with tonight's auction. Thank you again and have a wonderful evening everyone. I give you Sally Sudbury . . . '

Madame Ruby raised her champagne glass to her audience, took a sip and passed the glittering microphone to a terrified, yet remarkably composed Sally.

'Th . . . thank you, Madame Ruby,' she began, trying to steady her nerves and her voice. 'Welcome, one and all, to the first years' auction of prizes. But before we begin, I would like to offer an enormous, money-can't-buy thank you to each and every person here for their contribution to this evening's event. Everything and anything you see this evening, from the staging and décor to the food and drink, and the prizes and entertainment, has been donated by one of you and for that we cannot thank you enough. I'm sure you'll agree that between us we've pulled off one heck of an event!'

The tables erupted into applause.

'Go, Sally!' Maria whispered loudly. 'They're eating out of your hand!'

Sally was beaming with delight.

'So if you could take your seats, ladies and gentlemen, we would like to open the auction with a performance from L'Etoile's award-winning songwriter Miss Pippa Burrows, alongside the beautiful voices of Charlotte Kissimee and Sofia Vincenzi, and with instrumentalists Betsy Harris, Lydia Ambrose and Daisy Mansfield.'

The spotlight suddenly lit the staging behind her and the band struck up the first few chords of 'There's No Place like Home'. The lyrics were so moving that, by the end, there wasn't a dry eye in the place. Leading the standing ovation was Mr Emmett Fuller, followed by his fiancée Miss Hart and then the rest of the audience. Mr Fuller took the opportunity to lean over and introduce himself to Olivia Burrows and Uncle Harry – who, of course, had been strategically placed on the table directly next to them. *(Well done, Maria!)*

'With your blessing, I would very much like to nurture Pippa's career, Mr and Mrs Burrows. She is a musical genius, and I believe she has a phenomenal future ahead of her.'

Olivia and Harry were speechless. Pippa had, of course, told them all about Mr Fuller of Universal Music, but this brought the whole thing to life . . . her performance and now this.

'Wow, Harry,' Olivia whispered in awe. 'L'Etoile really does bring the stars a little bit closer, doesn't it?'

Harry nodded with pride.

'Well done to our singers and musicians. A breathtaking rendition there of Pippa's latest songwriting triumph! And so now to the auction and our first lot of the evening. Writing and recording time in the studio with Pippa, producer Harry Burrows and an advisory visit from the Head of Universal Music, Mr Emmett Fuller. Who knows, with their help, someone just might have a number-one hit. Who will start the bidding for me at £50?'

'A hundred pounds!' Emmett Fuller called out, getting a laugh from the audience.

'Two hundred!' Antonio Russo Vincenzi exclaimed, winking at Sofia.

'Two thousand pounds!' Big Al Parry shouted out with a big grin. 'Two thousand pounds for my Alice!' he said.

A gasp went up. 'Two hundred to two thousand in one jump! That's ridiculous!' someone muttered.

Sally was the only person who didn't bat an eyelid at the huge amount on the table. She felt like a fisherman feeling an enormous pull on the line. There was no way she was going to let this one off the hook!

'Thank you, Mr Parry – going once at two thousand pounds . . . going twice . . . SOLD!' she squealed in delight. 'To Mr Parry, for his Alice, for two thousand pounds. Congratulations, Parry family.'

Suddenly Belle Brown shot out from where she'd been crouching at the foot of the stage, armed with a cashier's tin, to collect the cheque. There was no messing about at this auction. The first years had a job to do and they were taking it seriously.

Maria and Molly grabbed Sally's hand as she reached down to where they were sitting for a sip of water.

'BRI-LLI-ANT!' they gasped.

'You've started something now, Sal!' Maria said. 'No one is going to want to look less generous than the last man. You watch. They're going to spend a fortune here tonight.'

Sally grinned, loving every minute of her new-found talent. She was a natural. Only Maggie Sudbury sat in silence, tears of pride running down her cheeks. She didn't think it was possible for there to be a prouder mother in that audience.

But of course there was, Story-seeker. Everyone's mum is heart-burstingly proud of their child, most of the time. That's what mums are best at!

The auction galloped along at a heady, dangerous pace, with each lot raising dazzling amounts.

By the time the hammer had fallen on the final lot of the evening, the Fitzfoster Diamond (*which, Story-seeker the girls had saved until last in the programme*) it was clear that the diamond had raised the most money of any single item. It had been helped by the fact that Serafina Marciano, Lucifette's beautiful but useless mother, was bidding furiously from her home in LA. The Marcianos had not felt able attend the auction in person after the humiliation of the Christmas Gala. They had made their excuses to Madame Ruby, donated a ton of movie and music memorabilia and sent their long-suffering PA, Elodie Wyatt, to bid for other prizes on their behalf, while they barked orders at her down the phone.

Serafina Marciano, Story-seeker, was ADDICTED to diamonds. The truth was, when she received the auction programme and spotted the eight-carat, flawless Fitzfoster solitaire necklace, she knew she just had to have it.

Brian Fitzfoster listened as the bidding went up and up for his solitaire. He was the only person in the room who really knew its true value – and although it was a ridiculous sum of money, he couldn't help hoping those hideous Marcianos would pay more than they would have done had they simply marched into his Mayfair store. It was for a good cause, after all! Very quickly a plan began to formulate and he whispered to Harry Burrows to start bidding for the diamond, promising to pay every penny on Harry's behalf should he be left with it. Mr Fitzfoster was confident that Serafina Marciano wouldn't, and more importantly *couldn't,* let it go.

'Selling then to Serafina Marciano for the sum of one hundred and twenty-five thousand pounds,' Sally had announced confidently. 'Going once . . . going . . . '

'One hundred and fifty thousand pounds!' Harry Burrows suddenly leapt up, as though he was in a film or something.

'And we have a new bidder. Thank you, Mr Burrows.'

Pippa and her mum nearly fell off their chairs in shock.

'What are you doing? Harry!' Olivia Burrows asked, her eyes bulging in horror.

'Going once . . . going twice . . . for one hundred and fifty thousand pounds to Mr Burrows . . . '

'TWO HUNDRED THOUSAND POUNDS!' Elodie Wyatt screamed, echoing the same screech coming down the phone at her.

The audience was silent. Even Sally held her breath. Harry looked at Brian Fitzfoster, who shook his head and grinned.

'Mr Burrows?' Sally asked, but only because she had to.

'Congratulations, Mrs Marciano,' Harry said and

started clapping until the whole room was whooping and cheering.

'SOLD to Mrs Serafina Marciano for two hundred thousand pounds.'

Through the din, Harry leaned over to Brian Fitzfoster. 'How did I do?' he asked.

'Perfect, Burrows, perfect. The Marcianos are now the proud owners of a diamond they could have bought in any Fitzfoster store for one hundred and twenty-five thousand pounds,' he winked.

Harry gasped. 'Did she really just pay seventy-five thousand too much? Wow! Well, they do say diamonds are a girl's best friend! Thank goodness dogs are a man's best friend. Far more economical!'

As Belle collected the last cheque of the evening from an exhausted and slightly tipsy Elodie Wyatt, she noticed people whispering and turning around to the entrance to the auction site.

'LET ME THROUGH, I SAY!' a voice boomed across the crowd.

Molly, Maria, Pippa and Sally were piled on each other's laps, making the most of the spare seat at their parents' table – reliving the auction and trying to add up how much money they'd made.

'Oy!'

Molly's ears pricked up. She knew that voice. 'Calum,' she breathed, pushing the girls off the chair so she could stand on the seat and see what was going on.

It was him! Calum was there! 'CALUM!' she squealed, jumping to the ground and running over to his rescue.

'It's all right . . . leave him . . . I said it's all right!' she shouted to the security guards. 'He's . . . he's with us!'

Calum stood before Molly in all his grubby glory. He hadn't changed a bit – literally hadn't changed. He was still sporting the same filthy clothes, long, tangled beard and his face was grubbier and pudgier than ever.

'Calum, you came!' Molly exclaimed, not considering how he knew about the event or even how he'd got there with no money for transport.

Brian Fitzfoster jumped up, only to be immediately pulled back down by Linda Fitzfoster. 'Sit down, Brian, and let this play out.'

'Everyone! Everyone! Can I have your attention, please?' Molly turned to face the room.

'Here you go, Moll!' Sally said, shoving the crystal-encrusted microphone into her best friend's hands.

'Thank you, HWTM,' she smiled at her friend.

'Everyone, please meet Calum. It was meeting Calum in London on a cold April morning that inspired me – and my wonderful friends – to hold this event for a homeless charity.'

As the room erupted into applause and people started to pat both her and Calum on the back, Molly felt her eyes prick with tears. Maria gave her a squeeze.

'May I?' Calum asked unexpectedly.

Molly looked up at his big, round, friendly face. He was so familiar to her. But then he would be, wouldn't he?

'Sure!' she said, handing him the microphone.

No sooner had she done so than Calum made his way on stage.

'I have an auction prize of my own that I'd like to put up for grabs.'

'Is this some sort of joke?' Madame Ruby fizzed to Miss Hart, wondering how on earth this stranger had even got through the gates.

'I would like to offer the contents of my coat pockets to the highest bidder. You will be bidding blind and I'll only reveal the prize when the gavel closes on the highest bid.'

There was a rumble of excitement. Each table was deep in discussion about this crazy proposition.

'No offence – but what could he possibly have in those pockets that I'd want or need?' Elizabeth Jinks's dad, Gareth, whispered to Belle's dad, Daniel Brown.

Given the sudden confusion, Miss Hart thought that she'd better step in before Madame Ruby exploded. As she approached the stage, she heard Molly asking Calum if he was sure this was such a good idea.

'Mr . . . er?' Miss Hart asked Calum, holding out her hand to shake his.

'Moss,' Calum answered calmly.

'Mr Moss. You can appreciate our trepidation at this point, given that the auction has been such a huge success. Can you please give me some reassurance that the contents of your coat pockets are of some value to potential bidders? It would be very sad to end this wonderfully successful event on a low, given that the girls have worked so hard to support you and their chosen homeless charity.'

'It's good,' Calum answered.

Miss Hart looked at Sally, who was poised for auction action and then at Maria, Molly and Pippa who flanked Calum.

'OK then, Mr Moss. Sally, over to you.'

'Ladies and gentlemen, it seems we have a last-minute auction prize from Mr Calum Moss. You are bidding on the . . . err . . . contents of his coat pockets. May I start the bidding at fifty pounds?'

'Fifty pounds!' Harry Burrows exclaimed. Pippa beamed.

'One hundred pounds!' Helen Hart called out, much to the delight of the students.

'One hundred and fifty pounds!' Mr Potts shouted.

'Oh my goodness, the staff have gone mad!' Madame Ruby muttered. 'Oh . . . two hundred pounds!' she exclaimed and the audience clapped and cheered.

'Four hundred pounds,' Mr Fitzfoster said suddenly. Molly couldn't have felt more proud of her dad than at that moment.

'One thousand pounds,' Elodie Wyatt exclaimed with a *hiccup*.

'Can't tell if that was a Marciano order – or whether she's just had too much to drink!' Maria whispered to Pippa. 'Dad, quick – put her out of her misery. She can't afford one thousand pounds – I'm sure of it.'

'Two thousand pounds!' Brian Fitzfoster called out to Sally. A look of pure relief fell across Elodie Wyatt's face as she mouthed the words *thank you* at him.

'Do I have any advance on two thousand pounds?'

Sally asked expectantly. But there were no more takers.

'No? Going once . . . going twice . . . SOLD to Mr Fitzfoster for two thousand pounds.'

The atmosphere in the room was electric.

'Mr Fitzfoster, would you be kind enough to step on to the stage for a moment while Mr Moss shows you what you've bought?' Sally asked, still focused on the task in hand.

Calum began to empty his pockets item by item. 'And last but by no means least . . . this,' he said finally, handing Brian Fitzfoster a crisp gold envelope.

As Brian Fitzfoster prised it open, his eyes nearly popped out of their sockets. Leaning over to Sally to share her microphone, he read out loud: 'And the winner and their family go to . . . the Oscars!'

You could have heard a pin drop. Everyone was speechless, Sally included this time. Brian Fitzfoster stared at the envelope, unable to explain its contents.

Calum once again took the microphone. 'Ladies and gentlemen, I'm sorry for the confusion, folks. If you'd allow me to explain myself.' He turned to Molly. 'Molly, dear, would you do the honours?' he said, starting to tug at his beard and hair.

'I'm sure he just sounded American then,' Pippa whispered to her mum.

Molly reluctantly did as she was told and as she tugged, the beard came away, bringing with it a filthy latex mask which, moments ago, had clung to Calum's face.

'Oh my goodness!' Molly shrieked, slightly fearful.

'Blimey – this is turning into an episode of *Scooby Doo*!' Alice called out, making everyone laugh.

All at once, Calum pulled at his wild hair. 'It's a wig!' Molly said wide-eyed, not knowing whether to laugh or cry.

'CALAMITY!' Madame Ruby screeched, making her way on stage through an open-mouthed audience. 'Calamity – darling,' she recomposed herself. 'What on earth is going on?'

'Huh! It's Calamity Mossback!' Pippa squealed.

The news that Calum the tramp was in actual fact the world-famous, slightly chubby Hollywood talent scout Calamity Mossback, spread around the room like wildfire. Molly and Brian Fitzfoster were aghast.

'Molly, dear. I'm so terribly sorry for tricking you like this. You see, the day we met, the day of your Warner Brothers audition, the studio director had asked me to go undercover as a homeless person in order to do a bit of research before casting the role. I never meant for it to go this far, but how was I to know you'd go to such lengths to help?'

Molly had no words. As he put his signature thick spectacles on, she realised why she had thought he was so blind outside the studio. That part hadn't been an act, then!

'This sort of *fly-on-the-wall* behaviour is fairly normal for a casting studio when a script hinges on the compassion of its characters and the actors who play them,' Calamity continued. 'You see, Molly, the subject matter of the film is not dissimilar to your experience of meeting me as Calum and wanting to change my life for the better. I couldn't have dreamed meeting Calum would have had such an impact on your conscience and inspired you and your friends to put together a fundraiser like this. You truly are a wonderful person, Molly Fitzfoster, and many will enjoy the benefits from the money raised here today.'

Everyone was on their feet and cheering.

'I am also delighted to tell you that in honour of L'Etoile's charity work here this evening, Warner Brothers have agreed to match the amount of money you have raised for your homeless charity, in effect doubling your total.'

'Oh my goodness,' Molly said, finding her voice. 'Thank you so much. That means we will have raised about a million pounds here this evening.'

Calamity Mossback flashed her a Hollywood smile.

'Indeed, Molly. And perhaps now would be a good time to congratulate you on landing your first Hollywood blockbuster role. I hope the film is a huge success. You deserve it.' He began to clap.

This was too much for Molly to bear. Too many surprises, too much money, too much happiness and she burst into tears. Maria grabbed her sister as everyone applauded her success.

Everyone except Lucifette, Story-seeker. Let's not forget her dreams of becoming Hollywood royalty had just been trampled. It had been a totally rubbish year for her at L'Etoile.

'And congratulations to the rest of you who had faith enough to bid,' Calamity said, once again addressing the whole audience. 'But in particular to you, Mr Fitzfoster. I hope that you and your family will enjoy the next Oscar ceremony along with the rest of the Hollywood stars.'

Brian shook Calamity's hand and took his seat; his girls firmly snuggled up under each arm. He'd never be able to understand the girls wanting to enter this crazy world of superstardom.

'Good evening to you all,' Calamity finished, handing the microphone back to Madame Ruby, who had no idea how she was going to follow what had just happened and round up the evening. *Thank you and good night* would have to do on this occasion!

18

L'Etoile, Where Dreams
Really Do Come True

'The bit I don't get is how he, as Calum or Calamity Mossback, even knew about the charity auction. I mean, it wasn't public knowledge, was it?' Molly said in a puzzled voice, as she tidied away the mountain of make-up and hairspray from the night before.

'Oh, Moll – I didn't tell you, did I? You know when we were talking about whether Mum had managed to track him down, she said Eddie took her to the studio but Calum was nowhere to be seen. She made enquiries at the studio reception, explaining about him inspiring our auction. All she can think is that someone must have overheard her talking and told him.'

'No way! Talk about being in the right place at the right time!' Molly answered, hardly able to believe what had happened at the auction. Especially the part where she got the part!

'You're going to be a world-famous actress, Moll!' Pippa said, hugging her best friend.

'Yep – and you are going to be a world-famous singer-songwriter, Pips!' Molly answered.

'And you, Miss HWTM, are going to be a world-class HWTM television presenter. The way you held that whole thing together, Sally, was totally professional. You were a triumph!'

'Oh, girls. I'm so happy and it's all thanks to you!' Sally answered.

'All we need now is for Maria to be told that she's won that *Gazette* competition and our first year at L'Etoile will be complete,' Pippa said.

'Don't! I finished the article this morning, adding in the final diary entry of the charity auction – which sounded brilliant, BTW. I just hope Luscious and her editor like it! I'm hoping that the mini-interview with *Yours, L'Etoilette* will give it an edge,' Maria said.

'You're just lucky she wasn't too busy to talk to you, Maria,' said a grinning Pippa.

'Don't you worry about a thing, Mimi. If L'Etoile's

proved anything to us this year, it's that we're in the place where dreams really do come true. Even Twinkle would agree with that!' Molly answered, throwing her arms around Maria.

'Yes, look at all of us!' Sally agreed. 'We reached for the stars and got a whole glittering handful. It'll happen to you too, Mimi. You just wait and see!'

19

All Good Things Come to an End
... for the Moment Anyway!

'Pippa, sorry to interrupt your packing, but could I have a word before you go on your way?' Miss Hart said, popping her head round the girls' bedroom door on the last day of term.

'Of course, Miss Hart. Come in. It's only me and the girls here and I don't mind them hearing anything you've got to tell me — unless you'd prefer we spoke privately?' Pippa asked.

'Not at all. It's just — and I know it's the summer holidays so you may prefer to just have a jolly good break, relaxing at home with your family — but Emmett, er, that is Mr Fuller, and I wondered whether you would do us the honour of

♥ 178 ♥

singing for us during our wedding ceremony?'

Pippa thought she might explode with pride. 'Wow! Really? I'd be utterly delighted, Miss Hart. Nothing would give me more pleasure. I'll even write a love song for the occasion. I'll play it to you before the day, of course – just in case you don't like it!'

Miss Hart smiled. She hadn't known why she'd been nervous to ask Pippa to sing. Perhaps she was just experiencing the first of many wedding nerves.

'That's wonderful news, Pippa. And we'll love whatever you write for us. Thank you very much. I'll phone your mother this afternoon to request her permission and all being well, we'll send through details as and when we have them. There's still so much to organise.' Miss Hart could have chattered all day about the wedding but suddenly remembered herself.

'Now, spit-spot girls, time to get moving. Your parents will be waiting for you on the drive and I don't like the look of that raincloud. Have a lovely summer and I'll see you all in September, bright-eyed and ready to knuckle down to some serious hard work!' Miss Hart said. 'Who am I kidding?' she muttered to herself as she wandered up the corridor. 'Ready for some more mischief, more like!'

'How cute was that, Pips?' Sally said when Miss Hart had gone. 'And what an honour to be asked! They could have chosen anyone in the school and they chose you.'

'I know, it's so lovely!'

'SUPERCALIFRAGILISTICEXPIALIDOCIOUS!!!!' Maria screeched, holding her iPhone in the air and jumping up and down on the spot.

'What is it, Mimi?' Molly called out in alarm. Pippa gave her best attempt at a scowl at the use of her embarrassing buzz word.

'It's Luscious T!' she answered, tears in her eyes. 'They loved it, Moll.'

'Oh Mimi, that's marvellous. So does that mean . . .' Molly answered with a squeal.

'I won, Molly, I won!' Maria squealed. 'I'm in heaven. I must be. Things this good just don't happen – not to all of us at once, anyway!'

'They do at L'Etoile, Mimi,' Molly answered. 'You just have to reach for the stars and grab one!'

the orion star

CALLING ALL GROWN-UPS!
Sign up for the orion star newsletter to
hear about your favourite authors and exclusive
competitions, plus details of how children
can join our 'Story Stars' review panel.

Sign up at:

www.orionbooks.co.uk/orionstar

Follow us 🐦 @the_orionstar
Find us **f** facebook.com/TheOrionStar